D1714763

Happiest One!

Happiest One!

a novel by

D.C. Koh

To order additional copies of this book, contact:
Xlibris
1-888-795-4274
www.Xlibris.com
Orders@Xlibris.com
755113

ONE

Cold in Cincinnati in 1935

Grady

That better business.

The start of all the trouble, if you was to ask me. I never seen the humor in it meself. Some of the customers find it downright insulting. Bewilders most people, the first time they hear it.

To make matters worse, he's got that Eyetalian accent. But he's one Eyetalian who's been out and about. Out West, down South, all over. Spent a good bit of his time down South, to hear him talk. So he's got that accent and the one from the other side he ain't never lost and, oh my, the funniest of expressions. Not always does he get them right, either. I can give testimony to that.

Better.

A customer asks him, ever so politely, mind you, "How are you today, Felix?" and as likely as not Felix answers them, says "Better."

Well, no one knows how to take him. Is he bein' a smart one? Is he bein' funny?

Those that know the man, they know he likes to play. Carries on like one of the Marx Brothers. Funny part of it is, many's a time I thought to meself how much he favors that one they call Groucho.

And if the customer doesn't understand, why, Felix's laughing all the harder. He's laughing so hard it's a wonder me bar isn't shakin'. Oh, he gets a big kick out of it. To him, it's all a big joke.

So I let it go on. I figger no harm done. Some of the customers, the regulars in pa'tic'lar, they like him very well, they do. Not a bit stingy when it comes to buying a round, unlike some others I could name.

But I never figgered O'Toole. This I confess is a failing on me part. I should have seen it coming, bein's I'm in the bar business and a student of human natures besides. But I didn't; I don't think any one of us did.

But we all *should* have seen it coming, me especially. We all should have known that sooner or later some damn fool as big a damn fool as that little Eyetalian would take exception. But Jesus Mother of God, how could I, how could anybody, know that O'Toole would be the one to make trouble?

Jimmy O' is, what would you say? Seventy-five, a hundred pounds heavier? And what, a half a foot taller? At the very least. A big son of a bitch, I know that. Felix is a man of medium height. Slim.

Who among us would ever guess the two of them would mix it up? And who with their wits about them could say it would end the way it did?

I seen it all with me own eyes. I had better than a front-row seat. I had the best seat in the house. Before all the fireworks started I grabbed one of those crates over there and stood atop it. I was *this close* when their fists were a-flyin' — I could have been the referee. I didn't miss a punch.

But I'm gettin' ahead of meself.

On this pa'tic'lar night Felix makes his grand entrance with a new one I ain't seen around before. You can't miss him when he walks in. He's a very dark-complected man, has a thin little mustache. Dresses good. Makes good money so he can afford it. In a suit and tie tonight.

Told me later they went to see some comedy picture. Clark Gable and Myrna Loy. He didn't like it. He doesn't like comedies. "I doan fancy that stuff," he often says to me. He likes the cowboy pictures, Tom Mix and that shoot-'em-up stuff. The Westerns. They're his idea of a real show.

I would have thought just the opposite. Because he's such a character hisself, he is. I know he still has trouble with his English. I know that all too well. I'm sure he doesn't understand the jokes. I have no doubts whatsoever about that. Just as some don't understand him *or* his little jokes.

Oh, and the love stories. He doesn't like those either. Claims they're all a fake. He doesn't go in for the comedies or the love stories. Claims it's all made up. I know what he means by that all right. Felix, he has a mind of his own, but we are of one mind on that subject. I guess he has been as-they-say unlucky in love. Says Clark Gable's comical.

He confided in me wunst how the moving pictures helped him with his English, when he first came over from the other side. A nickel they were, back then. They're a quarter now. Boy, he doesn't think much of that!

"The idea!" he says to me every so often. "When I first came to this country, I could go to the show for a nickel. *A nickel!* Have a swell time and when I come home still have some change in ma pocket. Henry, tell me some: What's this country coming to?"

Many's a time he told me how when he first come over he went to the picture show every night. That's where he learned to speak English and act American. Hollywood taught him.

Still and all he's a man with his own way.

"Felicissimo!" I called out when he took a seat at the bar. He told me in the Eyetalian language that means happiest, and he's Felicissimo, the happiest one. It suits him. My, yes.

"How are you tonight?" I said and I could see it coming.

"Why, better," he says. "Of course!"

Of course.

"Hah!" I said, playing along, you know. "You always say that. *Better.* Keep your money, Felicissimo. I owe you from the last time. This one the house pays for." So I got him a bottle of his favorite and I poured a glass. Oh, he's a gen'leman. Always has to have a glass.

"House'll buy for anybody," some drunk I don't reccanize shoots his mouth off, on the way out. Good riddance, I say to that type.

That's when Jimmy O' puts his two cents in. He ought not to have done it but he did so there you are.

"House buys for dagos!" he calls out. "Next it'll be the niggers!"

"Here, Jimmy," I yell over to O'Toole, "you have one on the house too." Set his draught down in front of him. "Like somebody just said. We ain't pa'tic'lar who we buy for." Making a joke and walking away and thinking that was the end of it. I wanted no trouble, you see.

But it wasn't to be. O'Toole, he won't let it alone. Takes it upon hisself to look over to Felix. Felix ain't paying him no mind. He's got his beer in front of him and a good-looking wench beside him. How he gets 'em, I don't know, but he does.

Jimmy pipes up, "I'd like to know just who the hell you think you are, Mister."

Felix turns around to look at him. He's all smiles.

"I'm the guy you think you are," he says. Right out of the moving pictures, that fellow. I swear on the Bible.

O'Toole keeps it up. "Just who do you think you're better than? Better than what?'

I quick tell Jimmy, "Just a joke between friends." Trying to keep peace, I go over to him to try to talk some sense into that thick Irish skull of his. "Listen," I tell him, "you be minding your own business. He makes a little joke, that's all. Says that all the time. *Better.* Means nothing by it. Just a harmless little joke between friends. He's a good paying customer, Jimmy. Just like you, Jimmy, a good paying customer. Lord knows we don't get enough of 'em."

That's how you have to talk to Jimmy when he gets in one of his moods. He can be the life of the party, but when he gets in one of his moods he makes good and sure everybody in the house knows it. Gets to be a surly son of a bitch.

I think he's follying me, but he ain't.

"Let *him* tell me," he says, loud enough to wake up the dead. Mother Machree.

Felix has his suit coat off. He's smiling when he ain't drinking or making time with his ladyfriend. He looks over to Jimmy, who's just taken a big swally to show one and all what a big man he is.

Well Holy Christ, then the little Eyetalian comes out with it.

"Jim-mee," Felix says in that way he has of stretching a word to make a point. "Hey, Jim-mee, cange you keep your nose outa the glass?" He says it and then, to make matters worse, he starts to laugh.

O'Toole can't take it. "You go to hell," he says, "you long-nosed dago red. I'll drink any way I damn well please. You wanna come over here and make me drink your way?"

"I doan know you," Felix tells him.

"You do so know me, you wop."

"Behave yourself," I tell Jimmy. I made damn sure I knew where me stick was, just in case. I call out to the bar, "Drink up, everybody! Next round is on the house!" It's cheaper in the long run, I know from experience.

Jimmy O', damn fool that he is, gets up, goes over to Felix. I went for me stick. Felix is still sitting on the stool. He's watching O'Toole now under those long lids he has. The man goes and smiles at O'Toole, which is not something I would have done as a man in his predicament. No indeed.

The whole bar is quiet, waiting to see what happens next.

"Sit *down,*" I tell Jimmy, "Christ Almighty —"

Then Felix puts his foot in it.

"Yeah, sit down, Jim-mee," he says. And if that ain't bad enough: "Before you get knocked down."

I never would have guessed it. As God is me father. But that Felix, he has nerves of steel, that one. He is all smiles. Full of devilment. Don't know no better, I suppose.

Jimmy, he don't wait a second before he's poking his finger in Felix's chest. "Nobody's gonna knock down Jimmy O'Toole!" he tells the little Eyetalian, but he wants the whole bar to know it. "What's more, nobody ever has!"

I don't know what that Felix is made of. He's smiling back at O'Toole. I ain't seen this side of Felix before. The Eyetalian's never given me a minute's worry.

"Jim-mee," Felix says, stretching, "you better stop, think whatchew do. 'Cause, bro-*thurr,* there's a first time for everything."

"You're all mouth, dago red," Jimmy says, but I can tell he ain't as sure of hisself as before.

"Go sit down, and behave yourself," Felix tells him like he's talking to a kid come in off the street.

"Drink your beer, Jimmy," I'm coaxing him.

"You make me," Jimmy says, to Felix. Oh, his face is quite red and it ain't just the drink although a lot of it most certainly is the drink.

"I'll make you and ten more like you besides," Felix says. "Now go sit down. Go back to your stool and drink like a man and behave yourself."

"You make me, dago red." Another poke in Felix's chest with his finger, harder than before.

"You heard what I said," Felix tells him. "Now doan make me repeat it."

"I just wanna know who you think you're better than," Jimmy says, "that's what I wanna know!"

"Doan holler before you get hurt," Felix tells him. Everybody knows Jimmy can be a whiny pup sometimes.

It's a sight to behold: Here's Jimmy O', a tall man, standing over Felix, who is a head shorter and many pounds the lighter. But giving it back to him like nobody's business. *Still sitting on the stool,* mind you, but not taking any guff from anybody.

"If you won't fight," Jimmy says to him, "shut your yap."

"Jim-mee," Felix says, stretching again, "you talk mighty big talk, Jim-mee." Still sitting he says it.

Felix raises his glass to drink, but Jimmy pushes it away. Now there's glass all over the floor. Beer too. Well, that sets it off. Felix stands up, for the first time, and it's laughable. He's no match for O'Toole. Nobody in the place is.

So what does that Felix do? Pulls out a clean handkerchief, dries his hands, taking his good sweet time about it, when all of a sudden, he clenches his fist, the right one, and *swings* on O'Toole. Oh, my, he connects, and how. Unbeknownst to everybody, Jimmy has a glass jaw. Maybe he was caught unawares, I couldn't say.

Jimmy's down, but only for a second. He gets up rubbing his jaw and oh, such a red face! The bar is laughing at him. Oh, the humiliation! Jimmy's always fancied himself a pug, another Jack Dempsey.

Well now.

Jimmy don't waste no time, throws a right. Catches Felix with a good one on the chin. The Eyetalian takes it, backing away. Jimmy wants to end it quick and throws another right. But he's too anxious. Felix ducks and Jimmy misses by so much you'd think he had another target in mind. Poor lad. Blame it on the suds.

But then, and this is the funny part, Jim drops his hand. All of a sudden. It's because the little Eyetalian has *stomped* on Jimmy O's foot! He's lost his balance, poor Jim.

Welll, Felicissimo doesn't miss his chance. Swings a hard left into Jimmy's belly and Jimmy bends over with a groan you could hear in Hackensack. All this, mind you, is happening very fast. Me bar is laughing one minute, all quiet the next, so quiet all's you can hear is Jimmy breathing. *Hard.*

Then with Jimmy bent over from his foot and his belly, the Eyetalian uppercuts him with a right hand and, jumpin' Jehoshaphat, does he land one. Back goes Jimmy. I mean to tell you, it's a wonder his jaw ain't in pieces. He goes backward four, maybe five feet and meets up with a stool and over he goes. You could hear his head hit. He ain't in no hurry to get up.

"You stay there, if you know what's good," Felix tells him, or "else you'll go ass-over-end again, *Jim-mee.*"

Me bar has become a crazy house. I can't remember such laughing and carrying-on. There's people clapping, people patting Felix on the back. What does he do? He goes back to his place at the bar, back to making time with his ladyfriend, like nothing whatsoever has transpired, paying no mind to the beer and the glass on me bar floor. What a man!

It's all over now. Everybody in the place knows it's all over. Jimmy is grumbling something, something about a fair fight. Poor lad is none too happy. One of his ladyfriends helps him to his feet and together they go out the door, him leaning on her, a sight to behold. Jimmy's not looking so good.

Where was she a few minutes before, I was wanting to know. Well in all fairness, nobody can do much with Jimmy O' when he gets that way. Who am I to talk? In all the commotion I forgot all about me stick.

I went over to the Eyetalian. "Nice work, Fee," I says to him and sticks out me hand.

"Hen-ree," he says, shaking me hand like he's thinking about breaking every bone in it, playing like he does, but still, he's got terrible strong hands, "you Scotchman you. I wanna tell you some."

I don't bother telling him I'm Irish. I give up on that a long time ago. Don't matter to him what I am.

The place is quiet now like before.

"Hen-ree," he says, stretching, so I know it's coming: "I doan wange you buy me no more beers, y'hear?"

He gets his laugh, even if his little joke's on me. Funny man, he is too. For a man who don't like comedy pictures, he's a regular comedian.

But he has a terrible temper, that little Eyetalian, a terrible dirty wop temper. I never seen such a temper. I never knew his stren'th, neither, nor how fast. Not a soul in here did.

Well I have now and I can tell you I do not expect to be seeing it again. Wunst was enough. Lucky I was they didn't bust up the joint. I made it clear to both the gen'lemen since their altercation that I won't tolerate such foolishness in the future. Fortunately for all concerned, I ain't seen them in here together since the fight, last week.

I run an orderly place, I do, no matter me other failings.

Felicissimo

Make no mistake: You find out pretty damn quick who your friends are in this world. Yeah boy. Liss to what I'm try to tell you.

You take that boy Johnny. Johnny the Greek, that's how I call him. His father, the ole man? The hot-dog slinger? He's a Johnny too. Came over in -fifteen or -sixteen, I forget which. Diff'rent Johnny altogether.

The son, this Johnny I'm tellin' you about, was a nice, polite boy as long as I can remember. Nicest manners you ever wanna see. Mister Felix this, Mister Felix that. Before tonight, shuck, we was best friends. Justlikethat.

We was.

Ain't no more. Tonight change all that.

I was walk home from the saloon with him and it lookt to me I could see every star in the sky, that's how clear it was, and we was two good Joes and everything was hotsy-totsy. Laugh and carry on, oh, we was have a swell time.

This Johnny was tellin' me how he wants to go to the night school, become a lawyer. I ain't so crazy about the lawyer business; to me, lawyer means liar, but that's me. More power to him, if that's what he wants. He does all right, to talk. The ole man might sling the hot dogs, but he has a good head on his shoulders, and I was think the son was a chip off the block.

So I tole him, "Come up to where I live and have a shot before we call it a night." Wasn so late, but I hadda be on the job bright and early.

Oh, he was all for. "Sure, Fee, sure." Din have to twist that boy's arm, to drink.

But after we got to ma place, went upstairs, open the door and sweetch on the light, I got the sorprise of ma life.

Man oh man. What a mess.

Right away I knew who was. Big Irish palooka. That bigmouth: Jimmy Somebody. Fellow I beat the pants off last week. There he was on the floor, dead to the world, blood everywhere.

Soon as I came to ma senses, I lookt to Johnny. Johnny hadda hold on to a chair to stand up. Couldn do no other way. Next thing I know the boy's knees was shake. I ain't lie, *shake*, that's how badda shape he was.

Shuck, I couldn blame him for that. I was feel sick maself, I'll be frank with you.

Johnny, he couldn talk for a minutes or two, but he finely spit it out: "Felix."

I thought he wand that shot; lookt to me like he could use. Uh-uh.

Come to find out, he says, "Felix," and the boy can barely talk, "I don't know you."

That made me pretty damn mad, but I din let on. I was too busy check that man there on the floor. Dead, no question about't. Shot in the chest.

After a while I spoke up. "Is zat so, Johnny? How come? You knew me last week. You knew me ten minutes ago. You mean to tell me you doan know me now? I thought you was ma friend."

Shook his head. Everything he's got shakes, it lookt to me. That boy was a mess, to be sure.

"Oh no, *no sir,*" he says. "I don't know you. You're in big trouble, my friend."

Had a helluva nerve. Call me his friend. Just that minute I was no more his friend than the man in the moon. I may be dummy, but I know that much.

"It's pretty damn peculiar," I said, "how you knew me last week and now, all of a sudden, you doan know me? How come?"

He could see I was get madder by the minute. I was watch him. Oh man, I mean to tell you, young Johnny was sweat. The sweat was *pour* down his face like he been work with his hands, insteada set on his backside all day like he does. He likes the school: That's his line. But it struck me funny how somebody who had gone to the school could be so stewpid.

Just 'cause you go to the school you doan haveta be smart about't.

He repeat-ed it. He lookt to me in the eye and he said it as plain as day:

"I don't know you, Felix."

Well shit on you. That's zactly how I felt. I surely did. All this time he was keep up that shake business. That made me stop and think, and that's when I got cole feet. I din know if it was a fit or what the hell it was. At the same time I was so damn mad at that boy.

Now he wanda talk. "I don't know you," he says. "I never was here tonight," he says, "and you don't know me either."

All right. I had enough. I was ready to sock him one.

"All right, you," I said, "repeat it."

"I don't have to repeat it," he says to me.

"Then shut your mouth," I tole him. Oh man, I was hot. That's not a good way to be, but he made me mad, chewsee.

"No I won't shut up," he says. Funny thing. I never notice before. He was a little shrimp of a fellow. I saw now that he was.

Says to me, "You can't make me shut up."

"Well," I tole him, "bro-*thurr*," I said: "I'll make you and ten more like you besides. And if you doan shut up, I'll sock you one just for fun."

"I'm not your brother," he says. Like I'm too dumb to know.

I tole him, "You're not ma brother, you're not ma friend. Whattadahell are you? What kinda man are you?"

"If you wanna go sock somebody," he says, oh, he's some talker now, some smart boy all right, he wasn liss to a word I was say, "go sock that brother of yours. Mike. He'd be a good one to sock."

He was a little guy, and he was a lawyer already, no question about't. Remind me of Mike, ma brother Mike, that way. I let him talk: I din let on I had the same feelin's he did, oh, long before this. I din say no more about Mike. Wouldn give him the satisfa'tion. 'Cause it wouldn be the first time ma brother Mike got me in Dutch, then left me to find ma way out. Mike, he was good for that.

Finely I tole him: "Johnny," I said, "you leave Mike outa this for the time beeng. This's between you and me. Mike, he ain't got a damn thing to do with this." I was hope it was true as I said't.

"Take it any way you want," he says. "'Cause you don't scare me." Talk mighty big for a little shrimp of a fellow. "But that's who you oughta sock. Where's that drink you promised me?"

I gave him the bottle and that damn fool was drink, hold the bottle with both hands, like a bear does, or a baby. Lookt to me he was in as badda shape as before. Still shake. Shake and drink. That bigmouth, I din care no more. He was three sevens.

I was think about Mike. 'Cause he had a key to ma place; he did and the landlord did. Them two, and me. Nobody else.

I had funny feelin's, to be sure.

As for fight, I never hit Mike no matter what he did to me and he done plenty over the years. I always tole maself, He's your brother, same flesh and blood as you, you should look out for him, not fight one another like cats and dogs.

I was no more gonna hit this Johnny than I was hit ma brother Mike. He knew't too. He knew me: He knew damn well I was no more keel that Irishman than I was hit him. That's why he was talk so smart. Knew I was need his help, need him to do the talk for me.

So I tole him again: "You knew me last week. When you needt fifty dollars," I said, "you knew where to come. You knew where to find me. You forget that already, ma good friend? That was last week, I suppose therefore it doan count? Is zat how you feegure, Johnny?"

"I don't owe you a damn thing," Johnny says. "Not now, not after this." Hold the bottle like a baby and talk big at the same time. "You're as good as six feet under right now," he says, s'more smart talk.

He got his mouth back, and I guess the whiskey was starda give him back his nerve. Lookt to me and said't, what was on his mind all along, I reckon: "The cops will say you shot him hours ago and then went out on the town. Then you used me as your alibi. *Maybe that's what you did.*"

He was a smart boy all right. Too damn smart for his own good, you ask me.

"Is zat so?" I said, after a minutes or two.

Oh, he was talk now. "This isn't the old country." (Like I was too dumb to know.) "They'll hang you," he says. "You've got one foot in the grave right now, but you don't know it. You and my old man. Two dummies."

Din respect his father no more than that. Shame on him.

"I'm not worried about your fifty dollars," he says. "If you were smarter," he says, "you wouldn't be either. You've got bigger problems than fifty dollars can fix. Even your dago dollars."

I saw red when he said that word: *dago*. He knew't too. He knew I was hate that word but he said't anyhow. Just to rub it in; act smart, show off. So come to find out, that's the kinda friend he was.

He knew damn well I never keeled that Irishman. I was cover him up with a blanket when his name came to me: O'Toole. "My name is Jimmy, I'll take anything you gimme." That's what he used to say, tell the girls. He wouldn say no more. 'Cause Used to Be is dead. The other night I shellacked him, but I never did anything to him up there in ma place. That was the end of it, there in the saloon. For me, was.

But this Johnny was make out like I was the guilty party.

All right, smart guy, I was think; keep it up. I can get along with anybody, but doan make me mad. You make me mad and our friendship is broke.

This Johnny wasn half the man the old man was. *Not half.*

"Get the hell outa here, Johnny," I tole him, "if you know what's good. Get out and stay out, before I sock you one. Because if I ever land one, brother, you woont wake up till Sunday. You savvy?"

"Yeah, Fee," he says, "but you wouldn't hit a man with glasses, would you?" Fix his glasses and laugh. I din see what was so funny, I swear I din. That laugh. Was sound like a nanny goat.

"That remains to be see, Johnny." I wand him to get out and doan come back no more.

He brought the bottle up to his mouth and, man, I mean to tell you, he took a long drink. Show off, I thought to maself. Then I took a second look and I guess he need't pretty bad. Still shake like nobody's business *and sweat!* Remind me of a damn hog. Drink like one, I know that.

I swear, I din know what was wrong with that boy. "Johnny," I tole him, "you better go see a doctor. See if a doctor can help you out."

He was too busy cough to answer me. Was cough his head off. He knew better: He knew he wasn supposeta drink like that. Shuck, that boy was no dummy. Smart aleck, to be sure. But he had a good head on his shoulders, *I thought.*

So out the door he went. Went hell-on down the stairs. Not goodbye; good luck; go to the devil. Not one word to me. All right. Somebody who's no more man than that I can do without their comp'ny. I doan call that a friend. After he left, I din worry about him no more. He was the leasta ma worry.

That hogeye, he left me with only a droppa liquor and I swallowed it. Tasted pretty damn good too.

With that Johnny gone, I had time to think. But that's when I starda worry. Mike, you bastard, I was think to maself, get madder by the minute, you never was worth a damn. Always some damn thing. But you went and fixed me for fair this time. Whattadahell did you do, you damn fool you?

If I was lucky, he would be up in his room, sound asleep. If he wasn there, oh, man, I had ma work cut out for me. He could be in two places. (Two places: Because I know ma brother, that rumpot; I know his way.) *Either* he was in some damn saloon, get cockeyed drunk one eye can't see the other. *Or* he was in some back alley, already in that condition.

There's plenty back alleys in Cincinnati, brother. Plenty saloons, too, for that concern. He'd be in one or the other, but I was hope he was in his room. I surely was.

This is ma oldest brother I'm tellin' you about. Michelangelo; Miguele. Signor Miguele; Meester Mike. *Big shot Mike.*

Michelangelo

Humphhumph. Damn good theeng I shot first, I know that. Damn good theeng. Could be Mike up there all shot to hell.

The police, the lawyers, the judge. They'll all want to know what the hell happened.

Self-defense.

That's all my brother has to say. Self-defense.

He can say a beeg fellow. *Somebody who had no damn beezaness to be there,* he can say, broke in. In the dark. This beeg fellow, he can say, broke in. Tried to rob heem, he can say, tried to kill heem. Somebody, he can say, who was up to no good, that's all.

Felice, he can make up some story to tell them.

He can tell them, he can say they fight before. Over some damn woman, he can say. Hell yes. Some damn woman was cause all the trouble. They'll believe that. Humphhumph. Poor Felice, he never gets a good woman.

First of all, first — of — all, Felice, he needs to get a good lawyer. Over here you can't just kill somebody. Hell no. Over here they have to punish you. The damn lawyers, humphhumph, they have to make money somehow.

If Felice is smart, he's a smart man sometimes, he'll take Mike's advice. *Self-defense!* That's what I'm gonna tell heem when I see heem. *Self-defense.* That's all he has to say to those beeg shots.

Felice, he's a hardhead sometimes; but if he does like I tell *heem,* he won't have any trouble. None. *Niente.*

But if he won't obey me, Mike, his brother, his oldest brother?

Well-hell, what can I do? Humphhumph. Accidents will happen. I wash my hands of the whole damn beezaness.

It's Felice's trouble now, not mine. It's not Mike's trouble, *no sir!*

To hell with that stuff.

C'mon now. Felice, he gets one year in jail, no more. *Less,* with a good lawyer. That's another theeng I'm gonna tell heem. If he won't obey me, it's not my fault.

One year, no more. Humphhumph. *That's not so long, one year.* What's one year between brothers?

"Hey, bartend! Some service down here. You forget about me? My name is Mike!"

Redhead Red

I was thinking about that scallywag when the phone rang and it was him. "Hello, you Redhead," he says. That's his name for me. Redhead or Red or Redhead Red. Never May.

"Where the hell've you been?" I said, kidding him. That's just how we talk, the two of us together. "You just get home from sparking?" Sparking. That's what he calls going out with a girl and you-know. He likes to spark.

But he didn't laugh. Didn't sound at all like the happy-go-lucky Fee I know. Something's wrong when Fee isn't cutting up and acting the fool. But then he told me the story.

Couldn't help but be flattered. Said I was the first person he called. It should have been the police, and that's just what I told him. Right away, I said, *before* they find that Irishman up there and draw their own conclusions.

But Fee wouldn't go for it. Sounded awf'ly low. I never heard him sound so low before.

Told me a young fellow, Johnny What's-His-Name, was with him when he found the dead guy, but this Johnny got cold feet and wouldn't vouch for him. As much as said Fee did it and was using him as an alibi. Said Fee could've done the dirty work and then gone out on the town and brought *him* up there so he could blame Mike, his brother Mike. Mind like a lawyer's.

He didn't know Fee. That right there should tell you. That's a joke. I could wring that Johnny's neck myself when I heard that.

Anyway, Fee said if this Johnny, a son of a bitch but a pretty smart fellow, thought that way, what would the flatfoots think? They'd lock him up and throw the key away. No, Fee said, the only way he would go to the cops was if Mike went with him. Mike was the guilty party and he was the only one who knew what the hell happened up there. Said *he* had a pretty good idea, because Mike was his brother, and he knew Mike's ways.

Oh, he got hot under the collar just talking about Mike and this Johnny.

(He's cute when he's hot. He's cute when he's not.)

I met that Johnny once. Just a squirt. Not much younger than me but already smart-alecky like Fee's brother Mike. That's another one. *Walks all over Fee.* Makes a sap out of him. And time after time Fee lets him.

He was going looking for Mike and when he found him, he was going to talk some sense into him and the two of them were going to the station house together in the morning and straighten the whole mess out.

I wished him luck. That Mike. I don't trust that rumpot from here to the corner.

If you need a place to stay, I said, but Fee said he had his work cut out for him. No argument there. He's as polite as pie, that man. "Thank you just the same," he said, and asked how I was.

I told him I had a good day. I did too; that was no lie. I was waiting for Roberto to bring the car around when he called.

I want to kick up my heels while I still can.

Felicissimo

First thing I did, I check his rooming house.

"He ain't been here since noontime and he owes me three weeks' rent," his landlady, she said to me. "You see him you tell him I want my money." I din let on.

I went to one saloon after another. Every saloonkeeper in town I bleeve knew him. "Oh, yeah, Mike. Sure, sure. He's a good customer all right, the best." Blah-blah-blah. I din care to hear that stuff.

Mike, he was a rumpot all his life and everybody was his best friend. I spoke to Zo-and-Zo and this one and that one. But everywhere I went I was get the same story: Din nobody see him. I went to a dozen saloons, maybe more, and it was get past midnight.

Still neither hide nor hair of Mike.

Poor me, I thought to maself. And I starda worry.

Finely I went to one dump there and the fellow saw me, shook his head and poind out back. There he was in the alleyway. Set his backside down on a stack of ole newspapers. Wear his long overcoat.

This ain't the first time he done such foolishness there. They knew his way all right. They knew me too and I told them I doan know how many times before "Keep an eye on ma brother." I told everybody the same thing.

Sure enough, they did.

You know how cole it gets in Cincinnati? Well, they thought the cole might do him some good and they let him plop his backside down in the alleyway. You midas well say they threw him out.

For his own good, I guess they thought. They mend well.

Daddy, that time he took his belt off and beat Mike with it, he mend well too. Everybody does, I suppose. Damn if I know.

That drink business. Mike was drink for as long as I can remember. Couldn stay away from. So ma daddy, what did he do but take his belt off and fan Mike's backside with it. Mike, he was a grown man, thirty years old, when this took place. Thirty years old, mind you. Couldn behave to save his soul.

A thirty-years-old man and ma daddy took his belt off and beat Mike like he did when he was a boy. *Worse.* I'll never forget't.

Felt bad for Mike, but what could I do? I was just a boy and there they were, two grown men. Mike, he was come home drunk night after night until finely ma daddy couldn take no more. One night Mike came home drunk and Daddy, he gave him fair warning.

Mike went along I guess two months, maybe more, no drink. Then he made his mistake. He thought ma daddy forgot.

Uh-uh, brother. Daddy din forget. "I promise you, and I'll do it," he tole Mike. Next thing you know he had his belt off.

Oh, he beat poor Mike terrible. I felt so sorry. But it din do no good. Din do a damn bit of good to beat Mike 'cause Mike, he just went back and did the same thing all over again.

That drink business. Couldn give it up. That's all there was to it.

He had no sense, Mike. Never did, for that concern. But he was ma brother, just the same. Oh you betcher life. He made me mad every time he was get drunk, no question about't. But I was always feel bad when he hurt hisself and he did every so often.

He was a mess when I found him. Had that big overcoat on, the one he wears all winter, rain or shine. I call it his trademark when he's sober, just for de'lment. Good thing he was wear or I bleeve he woulda froze to death right there on that spots in that back alley. I surely do. I ain't kid you when I say was cole.

So there he was, ma brother Mike, set his backside down on a pile of ole newspapers, *and stink!* Terrible. I doan blame them for throw him out. Had to, I reckon.

Funny thing, with Mike. He always was one to carry a newspaper. Anytime you saw him, he had a newspaper under his arm. *Socialista, communeesta,* I doan know what-all. His big ideas was come from the diff'rent newspapers.

And he was always busy write letters to this one and that one, just to let them know what he was think about diff'rent suhjects. His good friend *Il Duce.* Stalin. Ole man Roosevelt. People I never heard of. Thought he knew better than they did, I imagine. I doan know what was go through his head. Once in a while he was get a letter back. Was show't to everybody he knew and some he din.

Mike, he had a good head on his shoulders when he was sober and chose to use. No question about't. And work? You couldn find a better man to work. Could do two to anybody else's one. Was a pretty good skate too. Such times it was a pleasure to be in his comp'ny. Everybody liked him.

But drunk? Man, I mean to tell you. He could be mean as catshit.

But that was Mike's way: everything to extreme.

So there was Mike set in the back alley on a pile of ole newspapers wear his trademark, all hunched up like an ole man. Needt a shave bad. Even in the open air his smell was make you sick.

He reccanized me. Barely had his eyes open, but he saw me just the same. He couldn play possum with me, I'll be damned if he could. I was his brother.

"Mike," I said to him, "whattadahell did you do tonight? Answer me, because if you doan answer me, I'll leave you here and you can freeze your backside off for all I care. Serve you right too."

He wouldn look up to me.

"I'm seek," he says after a minutes or two. Play-act, that's all it was.

"Oh yeah, smart guy? You are, are you? You're gonna be a damn sight sicker by the time I get done with you."

Made out like his feelin's was hurt. "I'm seek, Felice. I have a fever. Don't you believe that? Here, *feel.*" He reach for ma hand, but I pulled away.

That was Mike's way to talk when he was cockeyed. He lookt up at me, but then his eyes starda close, and his head went back down. I keekt the sole of his shoe — not hard. Just a tap, to call his bluff.

"There in ma room," I said. "Did you think I wouldn see that mess there on the floor?"

Oh, he woke up then. Eyes wide open. He saw then I wasn fall for his foolishness.

"I feeks, I feeks," he says.

"You fix, hell," I said. I wand no parta his foolishness. "How the hell you gonna fix? That's ma home, brother. Ain't yours. Such as it is, that's where I live."

"He was a bad guy, that fellow."

"Doan I know," I said. "Doan make no diff'rence to me what the hell he was. He's a dead fellow now. You had no business shoot him dead."

"I told that guy — he was a bad guy. ... Don't you believe that? Humphhumph. I told heem —"

"You told him what? What did you tell him?"

"I told heem, 'Stop in the name of the law or I'll shoot.' That damn fool came closer. 'Identify yourself,' I told heem. Still no answer. Not one word. He was a beeg fellow, that guy. So I told heem again. Still I didn't get no answer. J'see, I told heem twice, that guy."

"That's when you shot him?"

"Humphhumph. What the hell could *I* do? I'm a little fellow. He's a beeg fellow. *Gigante.*"

Gigante, hell. "That's it, brother. You're a smart guy all right."

"Humphhumph. Felice, I ain't no crazy man. *Yes, I shot your pistola.* I did, sure as hell. He was a beeg fellow. I told you before. A beeg guy." Tried to make it sound like shoot a strange man in the dark in your brother's home and leave him there was the most national thing in the world.

"You doan haveta convince me, brother," I said. "I knew him. Last week in the saloon there I beat the pants off."

Smiled, I doan know why. Finely he came out with it. "Humphhumph," he says. Shake his head and smile. "Over some damn woman?" he says. "Poor Felice," he says, try to butter me up. "Poor Felice. You never get a good woman. Never."

That struck me funny. You never saw Mike with a woman. But he knows all. He's the ex*pert.* Anything comes along, I doan care what it is, he knows all.

"J'see, don't you? He came after me, but he was looking for you, that guy." Try to make't sound like I shot that fellow. "He was looking for trouble, that guy. Don't you believe that?"

"Doan mean one damn bit what I bleeve, brother. That's not the point."

Put out his hands, palms up. Damn fool brother a-mine, wasn even wear gloves. Tough guy, din even have sense enough for that. Put his hands back in his pockets pretty damn quick.

"I shot your *pistola,* sure enough. But I don't know if I hit heem. It was dark there, Felice. I got the hell out. Damn good theeng I know where you keep your gun. I had to protect myself, Felice. C'mon now." He was a lawyer too when he wand. He lookt to me, to see how I was take.

"Humphhumph," he says. He knew damn well how I was take. "What do I look like, eh? I ain't no crazy man. Was heem, or me. I'm just a little guy. He was a beeg fellow. *He* came after *me. To hell with that stuff.* He had no beezaness to be there. He was looking for trouble, that's all. Don't you believe that?"

He shut up for a minutes or two, but his mind was busy work.

"I'll tell you what I believe happened," he says. "Somebody killed that fellow someplace else and left heem at your place. *Yes sir!* I believe that's exactly what happened. That fellow was dead all the time. Somebody brought heem there, to make it look like you did the dirty work. *Sure.* That guy, I bet he had plenty enemies. Hell, yes; plenty. You weren't the only one. Don't you believe that, Felice?"

"Yeah, Mike," I said, "you tell that to the judge. See what he says."

"Judge, hell," he says. He wasn as drunk as he made out. Still, was drunk enough for that to slip out.

"Don't worry, don't worry," he says, "I feeks it up."

"Sure, sure, you'll fix it up," I said. "Did anybody see you? Hear you shoot?"

"*No,*" he says, like I was ask a dumb question, like I was insult him, "*no.* Nobody saw me. Nobody was there."

Which I knew was a damn lie. I'd been live there ever since I came to Cincinnati and people there was come in, go out all hours. I din like one damn bit on accounta that, but I couldn better maself. I had ma mind set on buy a house, and I had save ma money — not like Mike, here today and gone tomorrow; no sir, I had save ma money. Sacreefice here, sacreefice there. I had plans to make a family one of these days, and I almost had enough for what I want, but what happen?

Almost.

But almost doan count.

I was so damn mad and there was ma brother, that rumpot, the causea all ma trouble, set on his backside in the cole alleyway and tell me he was sick when he was drunk and then lie to me and expect me to bleeve and all this time I got a dead fellow up there where I live and I'm sleepy, I'm all tard out and I can't go home to ma own bed. I was pretty darn tard by this time.

"Felice," he says to me, "don't worry. I feeks it up. I been theenking. All night I been theenking. Do you know what I theenk? Here's what you have to do. You have to tell that damn judge" — he hadda stop to belch — "you have to tell heem self-defense. *Self-defense!* That's all you gotta say."

Din sorprise me. I was expect as much.

"Sure, sure," I said, "you fix every damn thing. You're the fixer, sure enough. You put me in a good fix, brother, I mean to tell you. Now you want me to go before the judge and lie for you. That's how you fix."

Oh, his feelin's was hurt then. I had insult him. We went back and forth in Italian. But Italian's not always quicker any more. It's not always the quickest way to spit it out.

"Who else knows about this beezaness, Felice?"

"Johnny. The Greek. The boy, not the ole man. The hot-dog slinger's son," I said. "Come to find out he wasn worth a damn. I had a few shots with him at the saloon. Got to talk, cut up and fool. Oh, we was have a swell time. Walk out together, was head the same way. I invite him upstairs, have a shot before he went home. He did all right."

"Will he go to the *polizia?*"

"Damned if I know." I din let on that boy no more wanda go see the flatfoots than Mike did. Birds of a feather.

"Humphhumph. He's a funny boy, that one."

"He thinks the world of you too."

"Humphhumph. He's nobody."

"Lemme fineesh what I starda tell you, will you?" Lookt to me like his feelin's was hurt. Play-act. I din fall for. Mike shut up then, and I tole him the story.

"He thinks you did the dirty work," I said, when I was fineesh. "First words outa that boy's mouth." (I din tell Mike what-all he said. Doan pay to tell Mike too much.)

His eyes got so big. Was wide awake now, after what I had said.

"Oh," Mike says, "he's a crazy boy. I know *heem*. He never liked me. I was there, he wasn't there. J'see, this fellow. *He was a beeg guy.* He came after me. I thought he had a gun too." Blah-blah-blah.

"But he din have no gun, brother."

"Well, I didn't know that. Humphhumph. There in the dark. How the hell was I supposed to know? He didn't stop when I said 'Stop in the name of the law or I'll shoot.'"

"Why'd'n't you go home to your own damn bed?"

"Seek." Put both hands on his belly.

"Sick? Yeah, brother," I said, "I imagine you was sick all right."

"You gave me the key, Felice." Like the whole night was ma fault on accounta that. "You don't remember? C'mon now. You told me, you said, 'If you ever need a place to sleep, go there. I don't care what condition you're in.' You tole me, you said, 'My house is your house.' That's what you told me. You don't remember that? You don't remember?" Came out with that hyena laugh.

That part was true. Mike, he always remembered what he could, to use against you when the time came. Chewsee, he wasn a stewpid man, not by a long shot.

He stard up again. Once he got stard, he was some talker, ma brother.

"I went right to sleep. Noise woke me up. Dark as hell inside. I knew, I knew right away sometheeng was up. Some trouble. Some bad beezaness to be sure."

"How did you know wasn me there in the dark?"

"Humphhumph. C'mon now. I knew it wasn't you. I didn't shoot then. I called out, I said, 'Felice, is that you?' When I didn't get no answer I got scared. *To hell with that stuff.* I quick, found your *pistola* in the cabinet there."

"I never move. I always keep in the same place."

"Sì, sì," he says. "Damn good theeng too. I checked the gun. There in the dark. Only light I had was coming from the street. Helped some, but not much. *Boom-boom-boom.* That's all."

"You wanda make good and sure he was dead, I suppose."

"What the hell? That beeg fellow, *he* came after *me*. Humphhumph. Fell down pretty damn quick." Shrug his shoulders like he just lost a bet on a damn hoss race.

Shook ma head. "But he din have no gun," I said.

Din waste no time. "I didn't know that, Felice. J'see he had no beezaness to be there. He came to steal, to fight. I didn't know what the hell that fellow was up there for. He wouldn't say one word. I don't know who he is. Don't you believe that, Felice?"

"I think you're a goddamn liar most of the time," I said. Sure, sure, I was bleeve him, this time. But I wouldn give him the satisfa'tion. There were so many other times you couldn keep account.

"Where the hell's ma gun now, brother?"

"In the river. Nobody will ever find it."

"Ma gun's in the Ohio River?"

"Sì, sì. I threw it there. Now you can tell the *polizia* you don't have a gun."

I was so damn mad I couldn look at him. When I did he was look to me worse than ever. He had icicles in his mustache and was some yellow stuff come from his eyes.

"Mike, you damn fool."

Shrug his shoulders and that boy always did smile at the wrong time. Make you wanna bop him one. Oh, he was a foxy fellow when he wand. But you could only do so much with Mike drunk. That only stands to reason.

"You damn fool," I tole him again. "I was think about you tonight. You remember that time Daddy took his belt off and beat you? For drink like a damn hog?"

Smile again. He din forget. But he din care.

"Let me tell you sometheeng, Felice. Felice, listen to me."

"I doan wanna hear no more outa you, Mike."

"Felice, listen, listen to me. C'mon now. Nobody knows about a gun. There is no gun. That Johnny, that Greek boy? The one who doesn't like me? To hell with heem. He can say to the judge, to the *polizia*, the lawyers. He can tell them all you were with heem last night. That's all."

Came out with that hyena laugh of his that makes me so damn mad. Said, "You have an alibi right there."

"I ain't got shit, brother. Din you hear one word I said? You fixed me for fair this time."

"No, no, Felice. Listen, listen. Listen to me, Mike."

"Yeah, liss to you," I said. "Every damn time I liss to you I get into trouble. Never fails."

He liked to hear hisself talk. Always did, for that concern. Talk, and drink. That was Mike's way. But he could do the work of two men when he wand.

"C'mon now. Listen to me, listen to Mike. I know just what you gotta do about this damn mess. Listen to your brother Mike."

I liss to him. Why, I couldn tell you. He was ma brother, the oldest. I guess that had some to do with't.

"What cange you do?" I said after he repeat-ed what he just said, oh, no more than a minutes or two before. "Mike," I tole him, "you have to go to the police, that's all there is to it." I spoke as plain as I know how: *"Go to the police and tell the truth for once in your life."*

Oh, a funny look came over his face. He din like that very well. That was the worst thing I could say to him.

"The *polizia?* Oh, no, to hell with that stuff. I won't do that. Humphhumph. What do you theenk, Felice? Do you theenk I am a crazy man? Humphhumph. *Polizia,* hell."

"Yes, brother, the *polizia.* You're acquainted with, I bleeve."

"Felice," he says, and now he was act again like I was the one who did the job on that fellow, "you have an alibi. You have all you need. Don't you believe that?"

"I doan have a damn thing," I said. "You threw ma gun in the river. That had your fingerprints on, not mine. I can't go home again. There's a dead fellow on the floor there. Did you forget?"

"All right, Felice, all right. Don't worry about it. I won't letch you down."

"All right what?" I said. "Spit it out."

"I'll go to the *polizia,* the *carabinieri.* I'll tell them the whole story. That's all. Self-defense. They'll believe that. *Sicuro.*"

Seemt pretty damn sure of hisself, but I wasn. *Sicuro,* my ass.

"I'll tell them, I'll say, 'Look at me. I'm just a little guy. He was a beeg fellow. He had no beezaness to be there.'"

First thing he said all night made any sense.

"You better sober up, first," I said, "before you do anything."

Nobody was bleeve anything that was come outa that mouth. Not look like he did; that only stands to reason. His smell was about knock you down, and he was need a shave bad. Needta clean hisself up, no question. But with Mike, chewsee, you could only do one such thing at a time.

"Sure, sure," I was try to encourage him, "sober up, wash up, put on some clean clothes if you got. Some sleep in a bed woont hurt you neither."

Oh we was best friends then. Everything was hotsty-totsy. He starda stand up. Him watch me, me watch him. He wait and wait till finely he saw I wasn fall for. *Damn* if he din get up on his own. He did't all right. Drunk but he wasn as drunk as he made out. Drunk or sober, he like to see how much he could get away with. Oh, he was a foxy fellow, Mike, make no mistake about't.

But, stand up, he was look bad sure enough.

"Felice, I have a plan." He was back to that. I doan suppose it ever left his head. "I'll go to my place. Clean myself up."

"Take a hot bath, brother. That's ma advice to you."

"Sì, sì." That fool grin, hyena laugh. "A shave too. To be sure. I'll go to sleep five, maybe seeks hours. Then tomorrow, *first theeng,* I'll go down to the station house. See the *carabineri.* Tell them all I know. The whole story. From start to fineesh. Every damn theeng."

"See that you keep your promises," I said.

"But first," he says, "I need some damn theeng to eat. Last night, when I came to see you? I was hungry then, Felice, I tell you. Don't you believe that? I'm starving now."

I couldn very well refuse him. He was cound on that. I had some money with me. I gave him a dollar.

"This is for food, Mike. Not for drink. If I find out you spend on alcohol, well, brother, our friendship is broke, I doan mean maybe. If I ketch you drink —"

"Sì, sì. Come with me, Felice. Come with me, to be sure."

I couldn do that and he knew. If I went to his place, it wasn that far from where we was, next thing you know somebody was show up at the door, look for me, ask questions. Lotsa people knew Mike, he was everybody's friend, and they knew we was brothers.

"That's not necessary," I said.

Had ma doubts as I said't. Thoughts was go through ma head. I wand more than anything, anything in this world, to trust him. After all was said and done, he was still ma brother, the only relative I had on this side, now that ma other brothers were all dead and gone. But I had ma doubts just the same.

"You go home, Mike. Get warm. Whatever you do, keep move." I was about froze maself.

"Sì, sì. I'll be all right," he said. I was surely hope so. He seemt pretty damn sure, but you can't go by that, not with Mike.

"All right," I said, "doan let me down. I mean it."

Finely we starda walk. I was hold his arm, steady him.

"I have a plan, Felice."

I couldn take no more. Stop right there in that spots. Let go his arm. Was about freeze ma nuts off.

"All right, you have a plan," I said. "God damn you, and your plan." I lost ma temper, chewsee. It was hard to keep your temper, with Mike. "I doan give a damn about your plan," I tole him, "the devil with your plan."

He starda say some, but I cut him off. I din wanna hear no more outa him. I had heard enough for one night.

"Shut up and liss to me," I tole him. "This is what we'll do. Brother, you go home and clean up. If you find some place along the way where they'll feed you, look-smell like you do, more power to you. Stop there. Eat till you bust. There must be some place open all night. If there is, you'll find it, if you're as hungry as you say you are. You know all the dumps.

"Me, I'll get a room some damn place, for what's left of tonight. I can't very well go home, and brother, I sure as hell doan wanna be in your comp'ny tonight." I was still mad at him, no use pretend I wasn.

Then he starda talk, so low I couldn make out what he say. Mumble. Make out like his feelin's was hurt. Play-act.

"God damn it," I said, "talk like a man, cange you?"

Spoke up then. "I'll see those *carabinieri* tomorrow. First theeng, *yes sir!* And now I'll get some food. Some sleep too. Then tomorrow morning, bright and early, I'll go to the station house. *Como si dice?* Spill the beans. Humphhumph. The very first theeng I'm gonna do, I'm gonna tell the flatfoots the whole story. From start to fineesh. Then you'll be in the clear and every damn theeng will be just like it was before. Humphhumph."

Look't to me then. His voice was get louder as he went along. Oh he was some talker all right. He liked to talk and he liked to drink. Smell to me like he shit his pants.

"Don't you believe that, Felice?"

"Brother," I said, "liss to me. Ain't no use pretend. I'm your brother. Ain't ever gonna be like't was before. Used to Be is dead."

"You'll see, you'll see. I promise you —"

I wanda go. "All right, Mike. See that you keep your promises. I'll see you tomorrow morning. I'll go with you to the station house, just so you doan forget to remember. I'll meet you around the cawner from your rooming house at nine o'clock. Your landlady, she claims you owe her money, so watch your step. Nine o'clock, now. Doan forget. Not before, not after. Doan let me down."

"All right, all right," he says, "I won't forget."

"See that you doan," I said. "You wait for me. Nine o'clock, around the cawner from your place. By the shoemaker. I'll be wait. You and me, we'll go down to the station house together. Face the music." Felt like I was talk to a small boy.

"All right, all right."

"Like men, like brothers."

"Sì, sì."

"And clean yourself up."

"All right, all right."

He went one way, and I went the other.

Michelangelo

J'see now, don't you? Your own flesh and blood. No better than a stranger on the street. *Worse.* Humphumph. When trouble comes, let, me, tell, you. When trouble comes you, can, trust, nobody.

You saw your own brother. Your own flesh and blood. You saw how he was back there. Humphhumph. Talk to me, Mike, like I was a dog. That's some damn beezaness, that is.

(Belch.)

Another beeg shot. Won't come to my place. Oh no. Mike's place ain't good enough for heem. That's some bullshit, that is. To hell with that stuff.

He leaves me. Mike, his oldest brother. He leaves me out here in the cold. Geeves to me one dollar, no more. Says to me, his brother Mike, he says, If I ketch you, we'll have a falling-out for sure. This is for food, Mike; no dreenk. If I ketch you.

Humphhumph. Some beeg shot brother I got.

Leaves me out in the cold, with one dollar. For food, not for dreenk. If I ketch you, he says. Mike, he says, tomorrow morning. First theeng. We go to the station house.

Sure, sure, Felice. First theeng, Felice.

Do you believe that stuff? Humphhumph.

Sure, sure, brother. I'll go to the station house. First theeng tomorrow morning. Before breakfast. *Like hell.*

Why should I go there? Humphhumph. I'm not the one who's in hot water. Felice. My brother with his one dollar. *He's* the one in plentee trouble, I'll tell you. He better know sometheeng, I'll tell you.

Humphhumph. What does he theenk? Does he theenk I'm a crazy man? Not for one minute, *not for one second,* would I theenk to go there.

No sir! I told heem what he has to do. But no, he's a hardhead. He won't listen to me, Mike. *So there.* I wash my hands. I wash my hands of this whole damn beezaness. How do you like that, Felice?

That guy up there. He was a beeg fellow sure enough. He had no beezaness to be up there. None, *niente.* I protect, I protect my brother Felice's home. I reesk, I reesk my life, and j'see the thanks I get out of it?

(Belch.)

One dollar, Mike, no more. If I ketch you, Mike.

Some beeg shot brother. You can, trust, nobody, that's all.

Your own flesh and blood are the worst!

Does he theenk, does he theenk for one minute I'm gonna go to the *carabinieri* tomorrow? And do what? Tell them, "Yes, sir, I shot that fool dead"?

Humphhumph.

Felice, the beeg shot. He won't listen to me. Says Mike, his oldest brother Mike, gets him in trouble. Humphhumph. That's too damn bad. Says, Here's one dollar, Mike. If I ketch you.

Ketch me. See what the hell I care.

(Belch.)

All right. I told heem what he has to do. If he won't take my advice, if he wants to be a hardhead, what can I do? I wash my hands. I told heem, I told Felice, I said self-defense. Self-defense, that's all you gotta say. That's all he has to say to the damn *polizia,* the judge, anybody who asks.

He can do that for Mike. After all, humphhumph. I reesk my life when that beeg fellow broke into his place. He had no beezaness there. I told him, "Stop in the name of the law or I'll shoot." He wouldn't stop.

Here's one dollar, Mike. For reesk my life he geeves to me one damn dollar, no more. For food, not for dreenk. If I ketch you.

To hell with that stuff. To hell with his one dollar. I can do fine without his dollar.

(Belch.)

This town is my home. I can sleep any damn place I want and nobody has a damn theeng to say about it.

Humphhumph. I have sometheeng, sometheeng right here in my pocket to keep me warm; plentee warm. Humphhumph.

I know where I can get another one too. And another one after that.

Here's one dollar, Mike. For food, not for dreenk. If I ketch you.

Ketch me. See what the hell I care.

This is damn good stuff.

(Belch.)

You know what I'm gonna do? I'm gonna sit down here, right here in this spot, and dreenk all I want. That's what I'm gonna do. To hell with Felice. To hell with those damn authorities. To hell with that damn shoemaker. *Ha-haa!*

Tomorrow. ... *Ha-haa!* ... Felice, he'll be mad as hell tomorrow.

So he's mad? I'm mad too. He's not supposed to talk like that to me, his brother, his oldest brother, Mike. Hell no. When he goes to the shoemaker and finds I'm not there, he'll be mad as hell. I'd like to see his face. Humphhumph.

When he comes looking for me again? You know what I'm gonna do?

I'll tell you what I'm gonna do. I'm gonna take his one dollar out of my pocket. And I'm gonna tell heem, tell Felice, I'm gonna say to heem, right to his face, "Here, beeg shot."

I'm gonna tell heem, "Here, beeg shot. You keep your one dollar. Mike don't need it. Mike has everything he needs, right, here. *Everytheeng.*"

Don't you believe that?

(Belch.)

Felicissimo

Oh, I found a room for the night all right. That part was easy.

I was so tard out I flopped down on the bed there, and the next thing I knew it was seven o'clock the next morning, the sun shine right in ma eyes. The first thought came into ma head was that dead fellow up in ma place. Ma brother Mike was the second.

I couldn ketch ma breath for a minutes or two after that. Felt like somebody had dumped a load of coal on ma chest. That was a damn funny feelin', to be sure.

Turn this way, turn that way but din do no good. I couldn go back to sleep. I hadda clear maself, that's all there was to it.

And I was determined to do so because, damn it to hell, I can go to sleep anytime, but I was never sleep like that again with some dead fellow, even if he was half Irishman and the other half jackass, on ma mind. I'd haveta to be dead to the world tard out or else like he was to get a good night's sleep again because that fellow, he wasn gonna go away so easy.

Uh-uh; no sir, no ma'am; he was not.

Genly rule I never go to sleep with all ma clothes on, but last night I was so tard out I did. When I woke up and saw that it struck me funny because I remember tellin' Mike to clean hisself up, and here I was in a flophouse, it was no better than a damn flophouse, and I din smell so good maself. Therefore, in the condition I was in, the circumstances, I was do no better than he was.

Worse, if you ask me.

Anybody can wash theirself, I was think, that's a small matter. So that's the first thing I did. The water came out of the spigot almost warm and I soap up ma face and hands real good and ran the water over two-three times and dried maself off the best I could. Felt a little better; not much, but some.

Just that one night and already I was miss sleep in ma own bed. When I came to this country the first time, twenty years ago, in -fifteen, I hadda sleep in a pipe one night. Just maself and two hobos. Just that one night, but that was one night too many. That was some I'll never forget.

I'm used to better; always was. You know how you get used to your own things? Well, that's how it was for me too.

I starda feel sorry for maself then 'cause I couldn go back to ma place. Not now no way. Later you will, I tole maself, after Mike tells the judge or somebody in authority what transpired. I surely would like to see that fellow outa there, first, before I go back.

No use kid maself: I doan bleeve I'll ever have the same feelin's for that place again. That only stands to reason.

I know one damn thing: I surely wish I had thought to get some money from there. But I was think about other things; I had a lot on ma mind. I wasn flat broke. Close to, but not quite. That's another funny feelin' and doan I know it. Doan I know it.

The bed, a washbasin and a night stand was all they was in the room. No meer even, but what could you expect in a place like that? I knew I couldn look so good, so I took a comb outa ma pocket and ran it through ma curls. I din wanna go out look like a bum. You never know who you might meet. Suppose I hadda go before a magistrate or some other big little shot? What then? I couldn very well look like some bum off the street. What kinda impraysion would that make?

Have Mike along will be bad enough, I thought to maself.

I had ma work cut out just get him to clean hisself up and I knew it. He's ma brother, and always will be, but you never know what that guy is up to from one minute to the next. He promised me, oh, I doan know how many times before. I'll do better, I'll do better. He does, for a while. For a while everything goes along swell. But sooner or later with Mike some always happ and everything is all shot to hell again. It's the same damn thing all over again.

Well, he promised me this time. (Like he did all the other times.) Let's see what he will do. He's made a liar outa me before, but sometimes he can keep his word. You can only hope for the best. That's all any of us can do.

I went down the stairs and tole the fellow there I was leave, but din make no diff'rence to him. Shuck, he was half-asleep hisself. I gave him the room key and out the door I went. Happ to glance at ma watch. It was about ha'-past seven. Close enough to call it that. Gave maself plenty time 'cause Mike's place wasn that far away. Neither was the station house for that concern.

With the change I had in ma pocket, I bought a newspaper from a boy and I went around the cawner to an all-night diner and got a hot cuppa coffee. While I was drink ma coffee I took a quick look at every page of the paper, try and see if they had some to say about a dead guy in an apartment. If they did, I din see.

That din mean much. *I* knew he was still up there.

The coffee tasted like it was cook-ed on fire and I left the diner feel hot. Felt good to be outside. I bought some fresh pears from a street vendor and I went around the block and found a hole in the wall where I could set outside, and I took out a handkerchief and a pocketknife. The coffee had hit the spots and I was still warm from drink. Kept me warm all right, and the morning sun was help too while I set there and et the pears.

I was enjoy maself very well. The sun was bright, the sky was clear as a bell. Not many people in the street chet and there wasn all that damn noise. You could still hear yourself think. After a while the birds, they came around for food. You couldn blame 'em, but I couldn give 'em what I din have. I had done et all my pears by that time, and I doan know if they would eat the pears anyway. I wished I had some bread, some damn thing. They gotta eat too, you know.

Ha'-past eight. Early, but that was all right by me. I wanda get stard. Anxious, I suppose. If Mike din show up, I would have to take a chance and go look for him. Lord Christ only knows what I would find.

It was fifteen minutes, not even that, from where I was to Mike's rooming house. Walk. I did before, oh, plenty times. Any trouble Mike got hisself into got back to me pretty damn quick, and if you knew Mike, you knew he was no stranger to trouble. Trouble was his middle name. So they knew me there too, thanks to him.

Was miss ma car terrible. I parked around the cawner from where I live, but was give me trouble so I put it up on blocks. That's how I left it 'cause I wasn quite done chet. I guess it was still there. Just as well I din have, I suppose. It din make no diff'rence because I gave maself plenty time to check on ma brother in case he din do like I tole him. Know him, he could be on the street some damn place. Chewsee, I had ma suspicions.

I tole one of the pigeons there, "Sorry, bud. You're too late. Better luck next time." And I got up and off I went. Walk.

Pretty day out as you ever wanna see. But cole? Oh man, made ma teeth chatter it was so cole. I only had that little jacket I threw over ma shoulders when I was look for ma brother last night. I was walk fast just to keep maself warm. Stop in here, stop in there to keep warm but din stop anywhere long. I wanda make time, chewsee.

While I was walk, I was think. For the life of me, I couldn stop maself think about that fellow. *Meester O'Toole.* Was a big Irish palooka sure enough. Bigmouth too. Seemt to think a lotta hisself. I beat the pants off him once and I would do so again if I ever found him up there in ma place, no question about't.

But, shuck, I'd never keel him or anybody else for that concern. Shoot him in the backside maybe. That's where ma smart brother Mike shoulda shot him.

I was wonder, What was go through that fellow's head? What did he have up his sleeve? Rob me? Keel me while I was sleep? Hell, what kinda man is that? What did he think he was accompleesh by that?

Funny people in this world, I know that.

When I got to Mike's neighborhood, what did I see there but prowl cars. Two, three, four; here, there, everywhere. Half-dozen flatfloots out front keep the crowd from get too close.

Oh brother, I was think, what now? I starda feel bad all over. Cole went right through me. *Either* Johnny, ma good friend Johnny, went to the station house and spilled the beans *or* Mike was get in some more trouble, some more monkey business.

I was hope it wasn Mike, but my belly knew better. I stood back a little way in the crowd there. Even so, somebody saw me, tap me on the shoulder.

Turn around and who was but this boy. Roberto; Robert. A pretty good skate. Cuban. Runs errands for Red sometimes. Always spoke to me, no matter where I was. Offered me a cigarette, but I shook ma head. I doan smoke but a pipe once in a while. Oh, a cigar now and then. But he always asks me just the same. A nice boy, polite. Spoke good Engleesh.

"Better go over and tell them he's your brother," Roberto was say to me. "You know what happened, don't you? *Que Dios tenga misericordia.* Didn't anybody tell you?"

He seemt to want to pretty bad. "I doan know a damn thing about't, Roberto."

"They found him about a half-hour ago," the boy was say, "right there on the pavement." Lowered his voice. "Froze to death." Pat me on the back. "I saw it all. They did everything they could. Tried this, tried that. At first they thought he just had one too many. But it was worse than that. They took turns slapping him till their hands hurt, first one, then another and then somebody else. But your brother wouldn't come to. He was too far gone. It was a terrible thing to see."

I guess Roberto couldn keep hisself from watch.

All this time he wasn look to me. Now he was look to me. "Maybe you want to say a prayer?" he was ask. "Maybe we could pray together?"

I shook ma head.

"You don't want to say a prayer for your dead brother Mike?"

I shook ma head and turned away from Roberto. "Damn brother a-mine," I said. "Stubborn mule." I din want to, but I starda cry then. Couldn help maself. He couldn stay away from, that's all there was to it. Goddamn rumpot never had no sense. In all the time I knew him, he never did. The firstborn, and the worst.

Still I would miss him terrible. When all was said and done he was still ma brother.

Roberto said to me, "You better go over there, Mister Felix, and tell them all you know. *At least identify him, he's your brother."* Oh, he couldn get over.

He din understand and I couldn tell him.

Minutes or two pass by. Sang a diff'rent tune then. He knew some was up. Said, "They've been asking questions. They couldn't find any signs of foul play," and he ask me if I knew what that mend. I said I did.

"When they found him," Roberto was tell me, "icicles were coming off his mustache. He had a bottle between his legs."

So there. After all this time know Mike, know Mike's ways, I was too stewpid to think to check, see what he had in that damn overcoat. I starda walk away. Away from ma dead brother too smart for his own good; Roberto; the police; all that mess. Felt like I couldn get no air.

Roberto came after me. Follow. I was afraid he would.

"What's the matter, Mister Felix? *He's your brother."* Oh, he couldn get over. "I know you got mad at him a lot, but don't you want to take care of him now? Now that life has passed from him?"

"Roberto ma friend," I said, "you doan understand."

"He's your brother," he said again, "that's all I know."

Starda lose ma patience, but I caught maself. I couldn blame him. I suppose if I was in his shoes I mi' feel the same damn way.

"He's still over there. They haven't taken him away yet. He's your brother, Mister Felix." Almost plead.

"No question about't," I said. "Is and always will be as far as that goes. But chewsee, Roberto, I'm in Dutch, and ma brother is causea all ma trouble. He was supposed to go with me this morning to the station house, straighten everything out. That's why I'm here. Now he's dead and I doan know how in the world I'm gonna explain maself."

Lookt like he understood. "I'll do anything I can, Mister Felix," he said. "You can count on me, Mister Felix."

Din know if I could or not. "One thing you can do," I said, quick, before he could change his mind, "if anybody asks for me, and I imagine they will pretty damn soon, I wange you to tell them you ain't seen me. Cange you do that for me, Roberto ma friend?"

"I'll do what you ask," he said, "but I wish you would tell me about it. Don't you trust me?"

"Whatchew doan know woont hurt you," I tole him.

"I'm not a bigmouth," he said.

"Less you know, the better off you are," I said. "Besides, talk doan do no good, Roberto. In this country you have to watch your step, same time look over your shoulder, make sure nobody is follow you. You make one wrong step and, brother, you have a lotta explain to do."

Roberto was twenty-one, -two years old but was still seem like a boy to me. His father came over from the other side; I met him once. Father and son, they was seem all right. Roberto, he knew what I was say. He was look to me in the eye now.

"Then you better get away from here, Mister Felix. Everybody in that rooming house knows you."

"You think they would blow on me?"

"You never know," he said, and I knew he was right. "They'll talk even if they don't see you. Can't resist temptation, most people. The flatfoots are everywhere. Somebody will talk to them."

"You're tellin' me," I said.

"All right, Mister Felix. I'll make myself scarce," he said, "so I won't have to lie to the police. I wouldn't run if I didn't do anything, but I'm one fellow who never does anything anyway."

I starda feel sorry for Roberto. He was too serious for his own good.

"Be careful, Mister Felix. I hope you change your mind."

No danger, I thought to maself. We shook hands and I starda walk. I din care where. Just get the hell away from there.

It was about nine-thirty by ma watch. I should be on the job. If I din show up in a half-hour, the big boss would know some was up. If another half-hour pass by, and he din hear from me, he'd send a boy out. If the boy din find me by noontime, look out then, 'cause that mend the big boss hisself would come look for me.

Pretty soon, I thought to maself, he'd have plenty comp'ny. Made me sick just to think about't.

Just that minute somebody goose me. Made me so damn mad I was ready to fight. Turn around and who was but Red. Out of breath. In that crowded mess there I could barely make out what she was say.

"Fee," she said, "you walk too fast. I'm so sorry. Come with us. I have the car. Roberto will drive us anywhere you want to go."

Redhead Red

When he saw me, his face lit up like a Christmas tree. "Hello, you Redhead," he said.

"Let me look at you," I said, and he said, playing the fool, "Lemme lookitchew first." Silly as ever. I gave him a great big hug and a kiss on the cheek, I was so glad to see him. Looked chilled to the bone, and no wonder. Cold as it was, he was only wearing a light jacket.

"I heard," I whispered in his ear. I didn't want to let go, but he shrugged. "Couldn be helped," he said. "Damn brother a-mine."

"I had a night on the town after you called," I said, "and a doctor's appointment first thing this morning. So Roberto hasn't had much sleep and he's had a fig up his ass all morning."

"That's too damn bad. What did the doctor have to say?"

"Just as good as ever." I didn't want to talk about it.

"I see," he said. He did too. Asked about Bailey, my so-called husband. A joke between us.

"Bailey's away," I said. "One week, Cleveland. Another week, Toledo. He's in Philly, this week. He thinks it's contagious."

Raised his eyebrows, smiled. He has the sweetest smile, that devil, even when it's forced. "Busy man, your Meester Bailey."

"To hear him tell it," I said, the two of us getting in the back seat. "To hell with Bailey. *Roberto,*" I called, *"back to the house."*

Fee, he patted my hand. No medicine could've made me feel better. But then he let go, looking out the window, lost in his troubles, his mind a million miles away from Cincinnati, Ohio.

It's about twenty blocks to my place. I can't take that much quiet. "I saw a marvelous show last night," I said, for something to say. "Just terrific until the cops came and shut it down."

Got him to smile. "What was? A dirty show?"

"Cops thought so, but they got a bum steer. Everybody still had their clothes on when they got there. Choogie Humberson's All Girl Revue."

"Kookie Humberson? Like the ice cream and kookies?"

"Choogie Humberson. The most fantastic kid. A looker, with talent. Sings, dances, tells jokes, funny stories. Wouldn't surprise me if she ended up in New York. Or Hollywood, in pictures. Put on a swell show."

"Wish I had been there with you to see't," he said.

"So do I, Fee honey, so do I."

Of course along the way I had to come down with one of my coughing spells. "I doan like the sound of that, young lady. Not one damn bit," he said, and I quick put out my Herbert

Tareyton. It's like smoking in front of your parents, anyway, when I'm around him.

When we got inside we sat in the sunroom. In the morning light he looked pale. "Can I offer you a shot, Fee?" I asked. He sure looked like he could use one.

But he said, "No, Red, thank you just the same."

"Maybe some coffee? Something to warm you up?"

"Nothing for me, Red. What I need is some help."

I thought to pull the shades. "Tell me what I can do," I said. "We have the car, and we have Roberto till five. After that he's extra."

Roberto came in from the street. "So what happened," he said, "that you can't go to the police and identify your own brother?" Snotty as hell. I wanted to slap his face.

"That doan worry me," Fee told him. "Lotsa people know ma brother. Somebody'll come forward. You, maybe."

Smart as Roberto thinks he is, he didn't know Fee was pulling his leg. Took Roberto by surprise. "Me?" he said. "Why me? When I saw Mike coming, I used to duck him."

"You," Fee said, "and plen-tee more beside." Fee went ahead and told the story. I didn't cry till I saw the tears running down that beautiful man's face. "That damn fool," he said and he had to clear his throat, "God rest his soul. When I stop and think, damn it to hell, it sorprises me it din happ long before this. Long before."

"Have a shot with me, Fee," I said. "Forget your troubles."

"I doubt't, but on second thought, I bleeve I will," he said. "Will this boy here join us?"

Roberto shook his head. He doesn't drink. Unfortunately.

Watching Fee sip his Scotch, I was thinking how much he wasn't like his brother. Mike was all about Mike. A damn fanatic. I'd seen him with people, arguing like a crazy man. And a mean drunk. One time I saw him pick a fight with a bartender who cut him off, and you couldn't blame the bartender, who was the sweetest guy. Nothing happened, but something could have. A man like that. He could turn on you at the drop of a hat. I'd seen him do it.

Fee didn't even look like him. "Mike, he was remind me of a dog I had one time," he was saying, and I took that as a good sign, him talking. Usually he's a happy-go-lucky somebody. I was worried in the car when he wasn't talking. That's not Fee.

"Peeto, his name was," Fee was saying, "prettiest dog I ever laid eyes on. Friend-lee? Too friendly, come to find out. You pet him, everything is fine. But you tell Peeto to come, he doan know you. Look to you, shake-a-tail, shake-a-tail, then *off* he'd go some damn place.

"Think you was play. Well, lemme tell you, I din keep Peeto long. Peeto and me, we pard comp'ny. Peeto found a new home.

"But that's a dog," Fee said. "With a rumpot brother, well, what cange you do?"

"You mean," Roberto said, "your brother was no better than a dog?"

Roberto was enough to try anybody's patience. Fee took a deep breath, wet his lips. "What I mean to tell you," he said, *"is,* in some ways Mike, he was no smarter than the dog. Now do you see what I mean?

"What you need —" I started to say, but bright boy cut me off.

"What you need is an alibi," he said.

"What you need," I said, "is somebody to stand up for you, somebody who'll tell the truth. Somebody you can depend on."

Fee shook his head, disgusted with the world. "Who would that be?" he said. "That snotnose kid I thought I knew him? Can't depend on that boy for a damn thing. Ma brother? He's dead and gone. Couldn stop drink long enough to help me out. Drag his feet even before then. The one who put me in this fix in the first place."

Threw back his head and finished his shot.

"First one today." He made an announcement out of it. Took his time clearing his threat. "That saloonkeeper, Grady his name is. He's scared of his own shadow. The police? Shuck, they'll draw their own conclusions. They'll make up their mind justthatquick, then lock me up and throw the key away. I need to get out of town. That's all there is to it."

Roberto nodded. He finally understood something.

"Where will you go?" I asked.

"Follow ma nose, I guess. To Jalopa, or some damn place. Can't stay in town, I know that. I'll need a new job, money to live on." Suddenly his face lit up. "Ma good looks can only get me so far, Red. Unless you know some reech widows. How about you, Roberto?" Fee couldn't stay mad at anybody for long. "You know any reech widows?"

"If I knew one," Roberto said, "I'd be on her doorstep." He really was just a kid.

"When you find one," Fee said, "get one for me too, will you?"

By now he was feeling better. His color had come back.

"At least we can still make jokes," I said.

"When we can't," Fee said, "we're in a pretty bad way. But no useta kid maself. I got trouble."

"Have another shot," I said.

"No ma'am, thank you just the same. Wuddia think I am? A rumpot like ma brother?" He smiled, to let me know he was kidding. "But you have another one, Red, if you think it'll help."

"It'll help," I said, pouring. "Next month I'm seeing a specialist, in Baltimore. See if he can help."

"I wish you luck," he said. He knew all about it. First one I told. The only one, for a long time.

"Damn shame, Red. Young girl like you."

"Don't worry about me, Fee. I'll manage."

"'Scuse me, then," he said, pinching my elbow. "I forgot what a tough egg you are."

He looked at his watch, then threw his hands up in the air. They landed on his knees, palms down, with a loud *splat*.

"Cheer up, Fee."

"Cheer up?" Shook his head. "Yesterday this time I was on the job, not a care in the world. Fix bad seams on teen cans.

That was ma biggest worry, and I was get paid for that worry. Today? Oh man. Here I am with you, try to get out of town before the flatfoots find me. Ma brother dead. Strange man dead in ma apartment. Cheer up," he said, "that's a joke."

Shook his head again, frowned, raised his eyebrows. His face told the story.

"I never in ma life went outa ma way to hurt the people, Red."

Roberto asked him, "What did that fellow want with you anyway?"

"Get even," Fee said, "*I guess.* Rob me, beat me, keel me, I suppose. But he never got the chance. Mike, he saw to that."

"Mister Felix," Roberto said, "if you didn't have bad luck, you would have no luck at all," and I was waiting for Fee to tell him to go to hell.

But Fee played along. "You're tellin' me," he said.

I'd never seen Roberto so excited.

"You'll have to tell us what to do," I said to Fee.

Fee was looking at us both with those eagle eyes. Some people say he has evil eyes. I supposed they could be, if you crossed him. I suppose they could be a lot of things. Sometimes I think they can see right through me. Straight to my soul, if we have such a thing.

"Thank you, Redhead, thank you very much. You too, Roberto. But I wange you both to be sure now. You could get yourself in plen-tee hot water, and I woont be able to help you out one damn bit."

"Maybe that's what I need," I said. "Some hot water. Maybe some hot water'll do me good."

When Fee smiled his whole face moved. "I doan wange you to get in Dutch." He was talking to me now, not Roberto. "Think a minutes or two before you say anything you'll be sorry for later."

Dutch, I thought. I use part of my house for a tearoom and I rent out my upstairs rooms by the hour to those who have no place to take their passion. Don't talk to me about being in Dutch. "I'm in," I said.

I was thinking: I wish I could get as much pleasure in one month as the girls that go with you get in one night. I should know. His brother Mike earned one reputation, Fee had another.

He caught me thinking. "Cange you tell me that smile is for?" he asked.

"Ask me no questions, and I'll tell you no lies," I said, and he *laughed*. He knew.

"You, Roberto," he said, "I know you're three sevens. Just barely. But liss to me anyway. If you're afraid of the dead people, some people, they are, you know, I doan know why, they can't hurt you; that's one thing. The flatfoots, I doan know if they're there chet or not, that's another story altogether. They *can* hurt you, no question about't. So tell me now, and that's that. No hard feelin's and we'll still be friends."

"We're wasting time talking," Roberto said. He was ready to go.

"Thank you, amigo," Fee said, and they shook hands on it.

He looked at me and smiled because he was remembering. "Nothing's changed since you were there last time. Right as you walk in there's two closets, you mi' remember, Red, one next to the other? The one nearest the door is the one you want. All kinda junks in it. Anyway, on top there's a box of pictures you can't miss. I took them over here, over there, everywhere. Ma mother's picture, the one I showed to you? I want that. To hell with the rest. Down below all that mess you'll find an envelope. Brawn. Bring to me. All ma papers inside. Should be two thousand three hundred and fifty dollars there too. Last time I cound was. I doubt that fellow got any of it, but cound anyway, to be sure. Every penny I have to ma name. So be careful whatever you do."

"You can trust me," Roberto said. He'd been trustworthy, so far.

"I *do* trust you," Fee said. "That's why I agreed to come up here with you and this young lady in the first place. I trust you both." He looked at me with his eagle eyes. "Cange you do it, Red, or not?"

"I'm having a good day," I said. "Just tell me what-all you need."

He needed shoes and socks, dress shirts, three suits, underclothes. You'd think he was taking a vacation trip.

"And they talk about women," I said. But that was Fee. Always wanted to look nice when he wasn't on the job.

"I wish I could go with you," he said. "Help out."

"Stay put," I said. "Don't poke your head outside the door. Whatever you do, don't answer the doorbell. Nobody should bother you, but don't be surprised if somebody does. People don't see the closed sign when it's staring them right in the face. Their passion gets the best of them." My hand brushed against him down there. "We know how that can be, don't we, Fee?"

Smiled so sweet I wished I had a camera. That was a picture.

"Before I forget," he said and reached into his pants pocket, "I bleeve you'll need this" and handed me the key to his place.

Before we left, I covered him up with a blanket. "Get some sleep," I said.

"I'll try," he said, "but I doan sleep as good as I used to."

Roberto

I do this for Señor Felix. I do this to help a friend.

It is very strange. All the shades are drawn. No one seems to be awake this afternoon.

Our Father, which art in heaven, I will be a happy man when this job is over.

It's too quiet. These walls are so thin but you hear nothing.

That business last night. I cannot believe someone did not hear it. I supposed in this neighborhood they do not often hear shots fired. I supposed they thought they heard a car.

Maybe they have secrets. Maybe silence is their code.

To think I could be a farmer in Cuba. A landowner. A man of considerable wealth. Over here I sweep the floor and drive this sick rich bitch all over town. She will go to hell one of these days. I won't drive her. I am not going in that direction. She has been driving herself down that road, all her life, if someone were to ask me. All her money won't save her.

I heard her, the rich bitch, tell Señor Felix that I cost extra after five o'clock. Like I was something to be bought and sold. One day the sick bitch will have to pay somebody to fuck her. Extra, because she is sick.

(I do this for Señor Felix. I do this to help a friend. But the capitalist cunt slipped me a ten-spot when his back was turned, and I took it. Clearly the job is worth ten times more.)

I will park a block away. This is the intelligent thing to do. Why take stupid, unnecessary chances? There's hardly anyone on the street, but an automobile such as this? Surely someone will notice it. An automobile such as this was made to be noticed.

If the police come for me, they won't care that I could be a man of property in Cuba. They will call me an accessory. This Redhead Red will be the same as me then. We will both be accessories, but clearly she does not care. Señor Felix could be as guilty as Judas. It would make no difference to her.

She's a brazen one and God has punished her for her many sins and still she will not repent. Hell awaits her.

Trusting Felix, Felix the Gullible One cannot see through her.

I would like to be as trusting as you, Señor Felix, but I never will be. Already I know more about people than you, a man of many more years than I.

You think of this as a Great Melting Pot. I think of it as a great snake pit.

Shit, I don't even like the weather in this country.

But you, my slow friend, you know something about life I never will. Perhaps it is that you know how to be happy. You yourself may not know the secret. But you have the gift of happiness.

How do you have it, and not I, who is clearly the smarter one? Is it because you are stupid that you are happy?

If Señor Felix were smarter, he would appreciate (as much as some other things, if all the stories are true) the way I have done this thing.

How I walked boldly to the front door and motioned for the *puta* to follow. How I fearlessly took the stairs to Apartment Two-H. How I knowingly took out a handkerchief and used it to open the door. How I swiftly understood the situation and acted decisively.

Señor Felix, that fool who wishes to be everyone's friend, would probably walk here, stopping along the way to talk to the dogs.

God damn it he stinks. My Lord in heaven.

Why does it not bother Miss Gottrocks? What they call a dame in the movies, even if she is sick from I-don't-know-what. Maybe she knows in six months, maybe less, she will be no better off than this fellow on the floor. Señor Long Fellow. Maybe stinking just as bad, or worse, before she goes into the ground.

But the pay, Roberto, the pay, she is good. Do not forget that. Even if it is a capitalist cunt's money. As long as she keeps her ungodly sickness away from me, I do not care.

I do this for Señor Felix. I do this to help a friend, stupid as he is.

But that damn smell.

The smell will bother the neighbors more than last night's noise. It will only get worse. Soon someone will complain. The landlord will come. Smart capitalist will remember to use the master key so he will not have to break down the door and incur the expense of replacing it. He will find the body. Call the police. All hell will break loose.

I should have thought of the stink.

We have to move faster. Time is of the essence.

Shut up now. You sound like someone in a stinking picture show. You are thinking too much. You are not paid to think.

Relax. The redheaded *puta* is doing fine. You are doing fine.

Perhaps you could do this kind of thing for a living. Lesser men have, some of them quite successfully. You could do it for a little while. You could do it until you know what you really want from life.

If you only knew what you wanted. If you only knew what makes a man happy.

If you only knew what Señor Felix knows without thinking about it.

Relax, Roberto. Nothing will happen to you today. Today is your lucky day.

All the same you better shake it up before your luck runs out.

I do this for Señor Felix. I do this to help a stupid friend in grave danger.

Redhead Red

I'll say this: Fee knows quality. What nice suits. What an orderly man too: I forgot how orderly. Takes care of his belongings. People who start with nothing, do. It's almost a rule.

I like orderliness, myself. It's a good thing I'm tidy. I try to be neat. When I smoke a cigarette, I try to be graceful. It's a good thing I'm smoking now. Fee wouldn't like it, but it kills the smell.

Roberto with his big old nose looks like he's going to turn green.

I forgot Fee had books. He's not a reader; he's a student. Italian-English. The government. Good citizenship. Arithmetic. Automobile manuals. Machines. Well, he's a mechanic. Works with his hands. His head, too, for as long as I've known him.

The Italians. What does he want first? What's first on his list? The picture of Mama, of course. With her face that looks like a man's. That's motherhood for you. That's what having all those bambinos will do for you.

That's something I'll never have to worry about.

Now the brown envelope. The brown envelope, please.

Better count it. All there, first try. All there, second try.

A man's life savings. I'm holding a man's life savings. My year's allowance back in the good old days when I was Daddy's widdle girl and I was going to give him grandchildren one day.

Thought I'd make a wonderful secretary. So some other man, *another* man, could tell me what to do.

Sorry, Fee. I can't get all you've got into this one grip. I'll just take down this small suitcase ... Fee, honey ... because ... you've just ... got ... too ... much ... stuff!

"HahahahahaHEHEHEhaha-uhuh!"

Oh, turn around, Roberto. It's not about you. You haven't got anything I want.

Roberto

Lead the way.

Open the door with the handkerchief. Wait a minute before leaving the apartment. Take the back way out of the building. Keep your head down. The *puta's* too. Put the handkerchief to your nose and blow, then fold it neatly into your pocket. Take a deep breath of fresh cold air.

Well done, well done. Bravo, Roberto. You're damn lucky you didn't puke back there. You missed your calling, kid. You should go into the cinema. Become another Edward G. Robinson. Or George Raft. Yet another avenue of opportunity.

All right. Don't pat yourself on the back yet. Walk to the car like you are husband and wife. Walk with a purpose. And what is that? To aid and abet in the commission of a crime, except in your Cuban heart you know it was an accident, a grand mistake, followed by more mistakes. But no one will understand. This is America.

Where *are* the people? Why is there no one on the street?

And now we are at the car. Finally. A much longer walk, with the baggage. Well, we can't be too careful, can we? Better than parking near the house. That would be asking for trouble.

Be a gentleman, Roberto. Open the door for the lady. Put Mister Felix's belongings into the trunk. Let the rich bitch who laughs over nothing carry the little bag. Whatever pleases her. Remember, Roberto, the pay is good and after five you cost extra.

Get in now and think pleasant thoughts. Tell yourself you are eating an ice-cream cone.

This is some car you drive. It is a pleasure to drive Miss Gottrocks's car, although it is no great pleasure to drive her. *But the car!* It is a car anyone would want.

Like her, I suppose. To look at her you would not think she ever had a sick day in her life. That's one hot mama all right. On her back I bet she is really something. *Was.*

Now, Roberto, it is necessary that you remain calm. All of this will be over soon. At least for you it will be. Think pleasant, generous thoughts.

Remember when you were ten years old and back on Grandfather's farm in Cuba and you did not have a care in the world.

Pretend it is a warm day outside.

Think what a great lay this *puta* sitting behind you was at one time.

Imagine owning this luxurious automobile.

What? What's this? My God, why hast thou forsaken me? Jesús Cristo!

Felicissimo

Damn if Red wasn right: People can't see what's in front of their nose.

I doze off, the doorbell ring. Doze off again, and sure enough the doorbell was ring again. Woke up a third time on ma own, but still was no sign of Red or that boy Roberto. Starda worry me.

But then three o'clock came along and I heard a *tap-tap* so quiet made me think a mouse was at the door and Roberto was whisper ma name and I let him in. Red was follow. Tickled me to see them. Lookt like they got everything I wand.

"You two kids," I said, "am I glad to see you! I suppose you saw that mess up there?"

Roberto, he coudn talk just that minute. He lookt to me to be pretty tard out. From what, your guess is as good as mine.

"Sit down, Roberto ma friend. Sit down and take a load off your feet," I said. "You too, you Redhead."

Din haveta tell him twice. That boy was all tuckered out. Red was smile ear to ear.

"Everything go according to plan?" I said. "You find what-all I tole you?" Some wasn just right.

"Everything was hotsy-totsy," Red said. She was smile, so I knew some was up. But I din let on.

"Glad to hear," I said. "I been worried sick about you two. All kinda thoughts was run through ma head."

Roberto was breet hard. That boy din get much extrycise, I doan bleeve.

Finely after all this time he spit it out:

"We broke down, Señor Felix. She stopped, and she wouldn't start again. That fine automobile." Sound like his heart was broke. "Three miles from here."

"We had to carry your suitcases," Red said and wink to me.

Roberto gave Red a dirty damn look. Said, "*I* carried your gear, Señor Felix. Everything you said to get is there."

"And then some," Red said, smile, and hold up the little suitcase she was still carry. "Some things I thought you might need."

"Poor Roberto," I said, "so that was the trouble? Red's pushmobile gave out on you?"

"I had to walk three miles," he said, sound pretty disgustopated. Gave Red another dirty look. I din like one damn bit, but that was between the two a-them, I had ma own trouble.

"Roberto had some bad luck," Red said. "He couldn't catch a ride for love nor money, could you, Roberto? But right away a nice genetleman took pity on me. Left me off a block away."

Smile again, to rub it in. *"Somebody didn't think traveling together was such a good idea."*

Roberto was right, I thought, but I din say so. I din know what-all had transpired between the two a-them and I din wanna know. I wand no part of it. Whatever it was Roberto wasn take so well.

"All on accounta me," I said. I was feel sorry for him just the same.

Justthatquick he stopped that funny breet. Seemt to cheer up. "Not your fault, Mister Felix," he said, which I took to mean he thought't was Red's. He was a stubborn somebody, no question about't. Moody too. Says outa the blue, "Maybe I should be a gangster."

Red and I lookt to one another. We din know what to make of it. Red was about to bust, laugh. "So this week it's a gangster," she said.

Gangester. I din know what he mend by that. I din ask. I ask him some I know some about. "What seems to be the trouble with Red's chariot?"

"If I knew," he said, "I would have fixed it myself." Sound pretty sure of hisself. "Save my feet, I know that. I probably have blisters."

"Keep your shoes on," Red said. "We don't need to see your blisters."

Roberto seemt to remember who he was work for then.

"She made a loud *pop!* and then she just stopped. That fine automobile," he said. Oh, he couldn get over.

"You can't go by that," I tole him. "Even the spensy car can crap out on you every once in a while."

"I let her drift to a parking place. I got your gear, and I walked back here." He wouldn look to Red. "It's a long walk, Mister Felix."

"Doan I know," I said, "I walk't a few times, from ma place." I had heard all I wanda hear about his walk. "Sounds to me like a connecting rod went up." I spoke to Red: "Maybe I should take a look and see?"

Oh Red, she got a big keek outa that. Laugh so hard.

Said, "Don't worry about the car, Fee. I can have that car fixed anytime."

I tole her it would only take a minutes or two, to see what the trouble was. "I woont even charge you," I said.

Made me feel good to see her laugh. "No, Fee," she said. "I can't let you do it. Too risky."

Made me feel funny, hear her say that. All ma life, chewsee, I was come and go as I please, answer to nobody.

Roberto spoke up. That boy had a lot to say, once he got stard. "Too risky is right." Was glad to see he was agree to some. Then he got real serious, and he said't again, "Maybe I should be a gangster."

Red and I look to one another, and *laugh!* Couldn help. This time I din care how he took't.

"Gangester?" I said. "Who you kid, Roberto? You're no more gangester than I am. No, ma friend. That's not your line. Mine neither, for that concern."

"That would be the life," he said. So serious. But wasn funny no more.

"Forget that stuff," I said. "Gangester. Whoever hearda such a thing. Keel, steal. That ain't no life. That's for the people who can't hold a job."

But he wasn liss. "I had it all planned out," and he sound like he was talk to hisself, "how I could get you out of town. With the car broke down, I can't even do that." Sound disappoind. I bleeve all ma trouble was a big adventure, to him.

"You leave that part to me. You done good so far," I said, try to cheer him up. "But *you*, you Redhead, I ain't done with you. I have a favor to ask."

Made out like she was a little girl. Pull down her dress. Bat her eyes. Made me laugh, forget ma troubles for a minutes or two.

Smile, laugh. "You don't have to ask, Fee. *You* know that." She was talk about some else, a joke between us.

"I ain't like some people," I said, kid her back, "*I* ask."

Red was take off her shoes. "As long as I don't have to go out right away," she said.

"You stay put," I said, "rest your bones. You already done plenty for one day. Question is, cange you let me stay here till it gets dark out?"

"You're safe here, Fee honey. You can stay here as long as you want. The cops won't come here."

"How can you be sure?" Roberto said.

"The cops won't come here," Red said again.

Roberto kept it up. "At least not right away," he said.

"I can handle the cops," Red tole him, and that was the end of it. Spoke to me: "So then it's settled. You're staying."

"Only till the sun goes down," I said. "I do'wanna wear out ma welcome."

"You can stay here on one condition," Red said.

"You're the boss," I said.

"You can stay," Red said, shake her head, smile so wide, "as long as you don't go out to fix any connecting rods." Hand to me the brawn envelope. "Your money," she said. "better count it. Make sure it's all there."

I did like she wand. Was no use to argue. I knew she cound already, but I cound anyway, to please her. That was Red's way.

It was all there. "All afternoon I been think about ma brother Mike," I said as I was open the big suitcase. "Mike, that poor devil. Can't go in the grawn with no clothes on, no matter how he came into this world. Here's what I need you to do, Red, when the time comes. Take a suit. This gray one here is as good as I got. This shirt. This tie too, I suppose."

Was laugh to maself. Even though I din ask for, Red brought the ties. I din expect that. Funny part of it is, I doan bleeve I ever saw Mike wear a tie more than once or twice in his life.

"Have the undertaker dress him up," I said. "But I doan wange you mixed up in it, Red. I just wange you to make sure it gets done right. Savvy?"

She nod.

"Now then, here's what the tombstone should say." I wrote down on a pad. Mike's full name. Born: Eighteen seventy. Died: Nineteen thirty-five. I din know what else to say.

"So chewsee, Red, you'll have your hands full. This next part I want Roberto to handle."

Oh, he perk-ed up then. Was all ears.

"I wange you to go see Johnny the Greek," I said.

Red spoke up. "Aw, Fee honey, that's a bad idea."

"The hot-dog slinger," I said, "not the son. To hell with the son."

"Blood is thicker than water, Fee. You don't know what that damn kid said to his old man."

"The son? That big baloney? He woont say a damn thing. He wand no part of it. No, Johnny'll do," I said. "If he doan, he'll get some respe'table big shot to do what I want."

Red was look to me funny. She din bleeve.

"Johnny, he's the only man that can do it," I said. "He's friends with everybody in town. All the good church people, they think the world of him. They ate a bellyful of his hot dogs over the years."

I tole Roberto a second time, "I wange you to go see Johnny the Greek. You tell him Mister Felix send you. Tell him I'm ask a favor. He'll do. I know he will."

"He has a big heart," Red said, "but I don't trust that son of his."

"I trust him all right," I said, "I trust him to be the louse he is. Forget about him." I gave Roberto five twenty-dollar beels.

"You give to Johnny. You tell Johnny to get an undertaker and a priest. Buy a plot of grawn. A tombstone with the words on this pad here. Tell him to keep whatever is left. He woont ask too many questions. But if he does, you tell him Red'll stop by and see him. You'll do that for me, woont you, Red?"

Red was smoke a cigarette. I hate to see that, especially Red, sick as she is. Try to hide't as soon as she saw me look. She knows how I feel about't. "I told you before," she said, "you don't have to ask." Smile.

"Thank you, you Redhead. Roberto, you understand?"

"I understand so far," he said.

"See that you do," I said. This was no game we was play. "I wange you to ask Johnny to take up a colle'tion for Mike. Pass the hat. That's just for show, so the flatfoots doan starda ask questions about who paid all the spenses and who did what. They can be nosey somebodies."

Red said, "If the cops come a-callin', what do you want me to say?"

"You tell 'em to tend their own damn business, and I'll tend theirs. How's that, you Redhead?"

"They'll lock *me* up and throw the key away. Not that I care."

"No they woont. Not you, Red. I seem to remember you have some friends in the *Po*-lice De-part-ment. I doan think the flatfoots'll bother you if you do like I'm tellin' you. But if they do, I imagine one or two of their superiors owes you a favor or two."

"More than one or two superiors," she said, "and more than one or two favors."

"That's what I thought," I said. "Roberto, whatever you do, make sure you give Johnny all that's left of that one hundred dollars. For his trouble."

"Yes, Mister Felix." Promised me he would do like I tole him.

I gave him ten dollars just the same. So he wouldn forget to remember.

"Thank you, Mister Felix. ... Poor Mike," he said.

"Poor Mike is right," I said. "Poor you and poor me too." I happ to look to Red, set there, with that damn cigarette again. "Poor everybody."

"What about that dead man? O'Toole?" Red was ask, try to help out, try to think of all that could go wrong and there was plenty.

"Can't forget that fellow even if I wand, Red. I'll take care of him all right. Best way I know how, under the circumstances. But first things first," I said. "First of all I haveta get away from here."

With that boy Roberto set there, I din say no more. I was take a big chance on him as was.

Redhead Red

"Do you need me for anything else?" Roberto was asking. "A stickup? A rubout?"

Boy's a scream. He had worked for me since early morning and from the way he was acting he had never walked three miles before in his life. But it was nice to see he hadn't lost his sense of humor, such as it was.

"Go home and rest up, Roberto. I'll be staying in tonight," I said, "atoning for my sins."

Had this sheepish grin. "You can't go anywhere," he said, "without the car." Seemed almost happy about it.

He was pretty quick: Even with that he could get on your nerves, but then he wasn't much more than a boy; I doubt he shaved more than once a week. He went over to Fee. Fee was trying to like him, but he was a hard one to like. He shook hands with Fee like a man and told him not to worry, he would take care of everything.

But he was no sooner out the door when Fee asked me, "You think he means it?"

"He'll do it," I said.

"How can you be sure?" Yesterday he would take my word for it. Now he sounded like Roberto.

"He's a religious boy," I said, making a joke. "I'll make him swear on a stack of Bibles."

"Think that'll do it?" Fee wasn't the same trusting soul I always knew; I wonder if he'll ever be the same.

"He'll do it," I said. "I'll make sure."

"Red's on the job," he said, being silly Fee. "That's all I need to know." But he was fidgety as he sat back in the chair, and he's not built that way, but who could blame him?

"Fee honey," I said, "let's have a drink on it. You and me."

"Sorry, Red, I can't." Then I guess he saw how hard I took it. "Maybe afterwhile," he said. "First things first. Before I do anything, I need to use your office."

What he wanted was a shave and a hot bath and his clean clothes that I'd just brought back so he could get on the road once it got dark out.

"I forgot to tell you, but did you happ to bring ma razor?"

"You could shave twice a day, those whiskers you have. How could I forget your razor?"

Smiled. "I din think you would."

"I'll run you a tub," I said.

"Thank you, ma'am," he said, stretching his words out like a Southern gentleman with an Italian accent. What a man.

While he took his bath, I stayed in the kitchen. What the hell, I thought, there's no law against it, and I got the bottle down and drank from it. I was cold.

My mother says I'll burn.

At least it won't be cold there.

She won't go there.

She told me so.

I got two clean shot glasses down and poured one for Fee and one for myself. I pushed open the bathroom door with my foot. It was warm in the bathroom. Nice and toasty.

"How 'bout now?" I said.

He looked at me and *smiled*. Old Fee smile.

"Oh you Red," he said. "You'll get us both in trouble yet."

"That's my middle name," I said. "C'mon, Fee. Don't be a stick-in-the-mud."

"Okay, boss," he said, "if you insist."

"I insist." I was feeling no pain.

Raised his glass. "First one to-day!" Storyteller.

We clicked glasses. "Who's keeping count?" I said.

He drank it down. He liked everything, in moderation. He cleared his throat. Blinked at me. Silly man, lovely man.

"You know what?" he said. "I bleeve that hit the spots, Red."

He made me laugh. Since the first day I met him.

Mother would never like him.

"Let me do your back," I said.

"All right, young lady, I doan mind if you do."

I took the washcloth and soap and lathered his back.

"Oh, that feels good," he said.

Sitting behind him, I took off my blouse and my brassiere. He knew it, but he didn't look back. He just kept his eyes down. I went to the side of the tub then. I wasn't wearing anything from the waist up.

His eyes got so big. I'll never forget that man's eyes for as long as I live.

(Maybe after too, but Mother says I'll burn.)

I brought his head to my chest. His head fit right between the two. It was like having three. I stroked his soft hair. What a pretty head of soft hair.

He raised his head and kissed the left one, then the right one.

My hand went in the water and found him. He doesn't feel like anybody else.

"There's that baby elephant," I said. "You should have a permit to carry that, Mister."

"Baby elephant's asleep, Red."

"I can wake him up," I said. "Unless he wants to stay asleep. Does my friend want to stay asleep?"

"Better had, Red. You wake him up, first think you know he'll get ideas."

He kissed them again. First the right, then the left. He liked to watch the nipples rise.

"You know best, Fee."

"Doan know a damn thing, Red. Noddny more. But respe't for the dead ..."

The dead are dead, I thought as I took my hand out of the water, and I'll join them soon enough. I bet they'd trade all that respect for one good —

"What a nice, old-fashioned man you are," I said, and it's true.

"Oh yeah," he said, "that's me. We'll do some other time. How's that, you Redhead?"

"Sure, Fee. I'll get a towel. At least I can dry you."

"That's what I call service."

"Maybe I can do something else."

"Maybe you can."

Felicissimo

Man oh man. For a little while I felt like I was on top of the world, din have a care in the world. That's what a good woman'll do for you.

I had Red bring me ma suit, clear shirt, and tie. Dress up. Ma dirty clothes I put together and I check here, check there, to make sure I had all ma belongings.

Put ma hat on. Overcoat. Scarf. Gloves. 'Cause you can't go on the road look like a bum. Even that first time I came over, back in -fifteen, and was flat broke; even then I was no bum. That time I din have no place to go and I hadda sleep in a pipe with two hobos; still I was no bum, then or any other time. No sir. You call me a bum and I'll pin your ears back, sure enough.

Went to the window and saw it was already peetch-dark. About ten minutes to six by ma watch. I took ma suitcases and ma grip and I kiss Red goodbye and off I went.

That Red, that's a true friend for you.

I had one foot out the door when I told her, "If you sick, Red, the hospul's the best place for you."

"Don't worry about me," she said. "You look out for yourself. I won't be there to keep my eye on you."

Seemt to me she always had her eye on me. First time I met her I turned around and there she was, set next to me. Quiet as a pussycat. I already knew who she was; made it ma business to find out, but I never intro*duced* maself. So now was the time.

"Hello, Maggio," I said, and she lookt to me funny. She din know what I was talk. "My name is May," she said, pretty snotty, seemt to me. "You talk pretty quick, sister," I said. "I ain't your sister," she said right back. I said, "Damn right, you ain't, you Redhead." Made out like she wasn look to me, but she was smile. Big smile. "You can call me Redhead if you want," she said.

So she was Redhead Red ever since.

I found a taxicab three blocks away and I took't to the train station.

All this time I had that dead fellow in the backa ma mind. Ma brother too, to be sure, but that fellow, *Meester O'Toole*, he wasn going away.

So when I got to the train station, I went right straight to the telephone. Thanks to ma brother Mike, I know some about the *Po*-lice De-part-ment. But just that minute, I couldn remember the number I use to save ma soul. So I ask the operator to get me the city *police*. She did.

I wait and I wait and I thought to maself, Damn busy people. They made me wait a good long time before finely some flatfoot came on the line. Greenhorn, I could tell right away.

Blah-blah Zo-and-Zo, he said his name was. Then I tole him who I was.

Spell, he said. I did.

I said, "I live at eight-six-oh-two North Kenwood Avenue, Apartment Two-H. To make a long story short, I came home last night, and I found to ma sorprise a dead fellow in ma apartment. Unless you know 'bout't already, he's still there to be best of ma knowledge."

I tole him what name he went by. He wand me spell for him.

"Spell yourself," I tole him. "I ain't no speller."

How the hell could I spell for him? He knew as much about't as I did. *Spell.*

Then he wanda know if I moved him.

"No," I said, "posateevely not. Why the hell would I move him? I din want anything to do with him in the first place. He was an intruder on the premises there I tole you and ma brother happ to be there by hisself and he din know no better, I guess, he got scare, and he shot him dead."

Din say a damn thing then. I thought the line was dead.

"Ma brother Mike keeled him," I said. "Shot him dead."

Well if I din tell that flatfoot once, I tole him a half-dozen times. Then he wanda know how I knew Mike done it.

"He tole me so," I said. *How did I know he done it.* I thought that was a dumb question to ask. *Stewpid.* Then I said: "Ma brother threw the gun away." Where? "In the river, that's where," I tole him. "He's dead too. Froze to death drunk."

So now then. He shut up. Din say boo.

"You can see to your own satisfa'tion what I'm try to tell you," I said. And I tole him where Mike lived and the street where he died and so on and so forth. He knew the whole story by the time I was done tellin' him.

Then he tole me, "You're a crazy sonofabitch."

Well that made me mad. Good thing just that minute he wasn stand in front of me and say that 'cause I'd be in jail and he'd be in the hospul.

I was just try to do somebody a good turn. Clear maself, to be sure. But it din make no diff'rence to me what some snotty-nosed flatfoot thought. I wanda clear ma name and at the same time I wanda let somebody — father or mother; brother, sister; wife, girlfriend — *whatever he had* know that damn fool up there was gone bye-bye.

"That's all there is to it," I tole the flatfoot.

Then he wanda know where I was. I almost tole him too. But I ain't quite as dumb as I look. Stop maself justthatquick.

I tole him, "That's for me to know and you to find out. *Smart guy.*"

Oh, you shoulda heard his talk then. He din like that one damn bit. *Smartypants.* I din care how he took't. I got cole feet when he ask me that and after I tole him to go to the devil I hung up the telephone. There was no more I could do nohow.

Soon as I got off the telephone, I took the train I wand out.

Oh, I had lotsa thoughts run through ma head, I surely did.

John Law

He was a crazy damn dago, and a fanatic, but I'll tellya what he wasn't: He was no troublemaker. Anybody that knew him would testify to that. Sure he drank too much, but all he ever did was make hisself sick with the stuff. He was harmless, perfectly harmless, drunk or sober.

Deserved better'n he got, *I'll* tell *you.*

Terry and me, we see worse, a damn sight worse, all the time. We knew him, and we let him alone. Like to talk about the government, here and on the other side, and I don't know if he was right or wrong. But he was one fellow that had a lot of conviction. Like most fanatics, I guess.

Michelangelo.

Love that name. Makes me think of the paintings in It'ly every time I hear it. Me and the mizzus are going there one of these days. Old Mike, that's what we called him. Seemed a lot older than he was. He liked to talk about the old country. He liked to talk, period. Even made sense some of the time.

Treated me and Terry swell. When he wasn't on a toot he'd give you the shirt off his back. He'd buy us a beer anytime he had it and times when he didn't. That's the kind of fellow he was, dago or no dago.

Sorry to see old Mike go. Damn tough winter.

Jimmy O'Toole. That's another story altogether. One of these days, I said to Terry many's a time. Or Terry'd say it to me. Hard to believe old Mike was the one that did the deed. I wouldn't think old Mike ever fired a gun in his life. He was the peaceful sort. Crazy, but peaceful.

Nobody believes that story his brother cooked up. And poor old Mike, he ain't here to defend hisself. He's deader'n a doornail. Just another drunken bum.

Talk about brotherly love. I guess we ain't in Philadelphia. That brother of his ran. *Ran*. That says it all. An innocent man wouldn't run. An innocent man wouldn't run out knowing his brother was dead, but that's just what he did. Didn't even have the decency to take care of the wake and such.

It took a good-hearted soul like Johnny the Greek to raise the cash for the final arrangements. Took in quite a haul, I heard.

Makes me sick to think about it. Running out on your own brother that way. What a man! I know I'd like to get my hands on him. Terry, he feels the same way.

That brother's got a lot to answer for, *I'll* tell *you*. He's the man of the hour in this town.

Grady

Oh, I told John Law he came into me place a right smart. Right after the picture show let out you'd see him. He'd come in and after a while he'd ask me the same question: "Grady," he'd say, "you got any quails on toast?"

And when I'd tell him no, he'd say, right uppity, he was taking his business elsewhere. Funny fellow. Never got tired of making his little jokes.

And off he'd go, down to the Greek's, to eat. He could eat, that man. I had occasion to see it with me own eyes. You'd never know it to look at him, what an eater he was.

Like a good many other things about him, we've since come to learn.

Skinny as an eel, he was. Quiet too. Too quiet. Then when he talked the words came out all wrong, or else it was too many of them. I knew he was headed for trouble with the law. I *knew* it. That business in me bar was kids' stuff compared to this. This is big-time stuff, this is.

Like I told John Law, when I think back to that right, the way he handled hisself, like an animal wunst he got started, I knew it was only a matter of time before he got in Dutch.

And so he did.

Well, nobody could tell that one anything. Thought he could lick the world. He ain't gonna lick this. I'll make book with you on that.

There's been talk about the brother, but there's no proof. Not now anyways. I didn't know the brother, but those that do, they say Mike, he was a talker, not a fighter. Nobody ever saw Mike fight. They say he liked to carry a newspaper, and whenever you saw him there was that newspaper, sometimes more than one, under his arm. Never a gun. That's some story, they say that is.

That Felicissimo. Shame on him. Telling stories on his own brother. He's miles away from here if he knows what's good for him.

Jimmy O'Toole, may he rest in peace, the bum. His mother and his girl come in here the other afternoon crying their eyes out. The girlfriend, especially, is beside herself. Tears streaming down that lovely Irish face. What she was doin' in the comp'ny of a mug like Jimmy I cannot for the life of me fathom. You can never figger what a woman will do, nor why.

The mother, and the girl, they're wantin' me to be in charge of the wake. Like O'Toole and me were bosom buddies, the best of friends. Oh, the look on their faces. The girl and the mother, such a distraught pair! Pitiful. They want revenge, and who can blame them?

I want to try and be a help. The fight was in me bar and I have a bad feeling about it. So I told them I would handle the wake, but for revenge they'd have to go look elsewhere. I ain't in the revenge business. I give 'em the name of a certain party, for their revenge.

But I ain't one to look a gift horse in the mouth. Have no fear, I'll look after the Irish lass. All alone in the world, poor thing. I'll give her me shoulder. Who knows where it might lead? Give it time and she might take a shine to an older, wiser man such as meself. Might go for me in a big way.

That Felicissimo may have done me a good turn yet!

Even if he is a fugitive from justice, a dangerous man wanted for murder, the very devil hisself.

TWO

Almost God's Country

Charles

You can go for miles on that road. After a spell think maybe you crossed over the line and went right straight to hell.

'Cause there ain't nothin' there. Bear, ever so often. In the winter you got your snow, and plenty of *it*. But not a livin' soul. Never nobody in the wintertime.

So sure enough, up ahead, in the middle of the road like he owned it, without even his thumb up, too proud or too froze for even that simple call for help, or else too dumb, was the poor bugger who was gonna make a liar outa Never. Which is just the trouble with Never: Soon's it's outa your mouth, that quick it becomes a damn lie.

That was my thinkin': 'Cause you never see nobody along that road. Nobody with their wits about 'em, nobody with any sense, would be out there. Only a damn fool would be caught on that road anywheres near sundown in the middle of Febbry.

So I tapped the brakes. 'Cause nobody, I don't care who they are, wants to be alone allatime, and you don't want nobody to freeze to death, even if it is some fool tramp. That's been heard of around these parts. Back in the woods you hear all kinda stories and they ain't all stories.

The man was walking slow, but steady. I put her in neutral and she braked towards him. Blew the horn and he turned around then. Blinked. Acted like he just woke up. Awf'ly good clothes for a tramp: for anybody.

I reached over and rolled the winda down partways.

"Hey, you!" I called over to him. "Wuddia think you're doin'?"

Blinked again. He made out the truck all right. He'd heard me. I stopped then and rolled the winda down as far as she'd go.

"You must be crazy," I yelled at him, "or else you got a hot backside."

Felt bad as soon as I said it. Closer I got to him, the more he looked like death warmed over.

"Mister," I said, "you might not know it, but it's a *long* way to the next town. Walking, that is. You best get in here before you freeze your nuts off."

That's just how I said it and I didn't give a hoot nor holler if he was a preacher or what. It just made no sense to me that a man would be out in that kinda cold. But there he was. Wore a topcoat like somebody's rich uncle. Hat. Gloves. Carryin' two grips. Surely he was no tramp. But a fool, now that's another story.

"Get in," I told him. "Hurry up."

You hadda talk to him thataway. He got in all right. Was funny to see. Moved pretty quick once he made his mind up. Didn't waste no time rollin' up the winda. Didn't need to be told that.

"Where you headed, Mister?" I asked him.

Puzzled look come over him. Didn't answer right away.

Finally he comes out with it. "Next town," he says. Plain as day.

So he could hear and he could talk. Peculiar accent. He don't look like or talk like anybody from around these parts. Had a real thin mustache. Wore good dress clothes. Shoes had a shine, once.

Thought he mighta been an actor; you know, one of them play-actors go from town to town with a show? You see 'em ever so often. Thought maybe he was an actor who missed the train out, or else an actor some town mighta th'owed out.

Then I had an idear he mighta had a breakdown, but I didn't remember seein' any breakdowns.

"Trump," I told him. Loud, 'cause I still wudn't sure he could hear all that good. "That's the next town: Trump." I hadda talk over the motor. Noisy damn thing.

Nodded like he understood. Sat there with his grip on his lap, another'n on the floor. Rested his chin on his grip and watched the road. Sleepy-eyed-lookin' fella. But I don't think he missed much. Took it all in.

"Go there myself," I told him. "Ever so often I do. Ever been there?" I asked him.

"Notchet," he says. "First time for everything."

He could speak English so's you could understand him, even with that peculiar accent. But he wudn't what you'd call a fast talker.

"Oh, I agree with you," I said. "First time for ever'thing. You'll like Trump. Lemme tellya, it's not a hot town, but it's all right. Ten miles up the road."

Less'n that, the way we was goin'.

"How long you been walkin'?" I asked. 'Cause he looked better, but he still didn't look so good.

"Doan know," he says. "Ma watched stopped on me."

"You're lucky I happened along," I told him. "Not much traffic goes by here. Yessir, you'da had a long walk on a cold day, cold even for Febbry. Colder'n a witch's tit out. Course I reckon you gotta expect that around here. You know where you are, don'cha?"

Looked at me funny. He didn't know where he was.

"You're right smack next to God's country now," I told him. "This is Western Maryland you're in. Not all that many live around here. They ain't found it chet."

Give me a big grin. He understood all right. Sat there with his hands locked together in fronta his knees and his chin restin' on his grip. Looked like a schoolboy. One who could mind. The kind I shoulda spent more time associatin' with so I wouldn't be drivin' no damn truck for a livin'.

It was a good while before the man took his gloves off. When he did, I took notice of his hands. They coulda been a boxer's, that's how big they was. Lots of calluses. Had the little finger on his right hand cut off b'low the knuckle. So he wudn't no more actor than me. You'd never guess it from them clothes.

"*Hey,*" I said, loud, 'cause I thought he might be going to sleep on me, "I know what you *could* do. Mizz Peele, Mizz Henrietta Peele? She takes in boarders. Has her rayglar people, but she still has room for ones just passin' through. Which might you be?" I went ahead and asked.

He shrugged. Made a face.

"Which might you *be?*" I asked him again. "Rayglar, or passin' through?"

Cleared his throat. He surely didn't talk fast. The man didn't do nothin' in a hurry, that was plain to see.

"Doan know chet," he says.

Honest answer, seemed to be.

I spoke loud and slow so's we understood one another. "Do ... you ... have ... money?"

Raised his head then. Got wide awake. "Surely," he says, "I keep all ma money in a rusty sock."

I hadda laugh. So he had a sensa humor.

"Lookin' for work, are you? You got a trade?"

"Machinist," he says, "that's ma line."

That made sense. 'Sides bein' tough, his hands looked smart, useful. Workin'man's hands. I figgered it out then.

"You must be headed for the packinghouse," I said.

Nodded. Says, "That's ma plan."

"There ain't much more than that there," I said. "Listen, if I's to take you to Mizz Peele's place, can you pay her?"

He looked at me. Devilment wrote all over his face. Nottatall like before. Finally he came out with it:

"You mean she doan take no wooden nickels?"

Made me smile. "Not her," I said. "Lord, no. She knows better. Seems like some folks is born knowin'. Not much gets past that woman. 'Nother thing I oughta tellya: You gotta behave yourself in her place. She won't stand for no monkey business."

"Oh, is that so?" he says.

"Yeah, that's so. Whatever you do," I said, "get that straight. Save you a lotta trouble —"

I stopped myself. I looked over't him and he had this big grin. I hadda laugh. He made you.

"Listen," I said, "you seem all right. You wanta go there, I'll take you to Mizz Peele's myself. That's where I'm headed. Take you right straight to the door. She has a lotta room. More room than she knows what to do with. Lotta room there just gonta waste. The old man, her daddy, he's dead. Henrietta, she runs the place now."

I know I talk too much. But when you spend as much time alone as I do, you *do*. We was gettin' closer to town. Saw some turkeys in the meadow.

"Her mama used to," I said, 'cause once I get started I can't stop, "but the old lady's in a bad way. Sickly thing. Henrietta has to keep her upstairs, locked up, outa harm's way, poor thing. Quite a burden on Henrietta.

"Good thing you ain't no actor," I told him. "Actors ain't welcome in that house. They had one awhile back. Bradford Munson, he called himself. Nobody ever seen him act, or do much else, 'cept spout Shakespeare and give Henrietta his undeevided attention. She wudn't useta that, and it went right straight to her head. This went on, oh, a good two-three months. Then one morning this Munson fella didn't come downta breakfast. Sent somebody up to his room. Called in what passes for the cops in these parts. But they never found him. He was long gone. Skipped out overnight. Didn't pay Henrietta a red cent all that time. Made it hard on anybody needin' a hand. Made Henrietta mean.

"So what with bad roomers and her mother," I said, "that woman's got her hands full. That's why I asked you what you was. I don't wanta to be addin' to her burden."

Outa the blue he says, "You should be good to your mother and your father. Everybody. I don't care who they are."

Well, that's the most he'd said all this time. He could talk good American if he didn't have that accent. But he made himself understood.

"That's the way I look at it too," I said. "I never did get your name."

He told me. Phillip or Felix. That accent.

"I'm Charles Hollister," I said and stuck my hand out. Man had a good strong grip. "Senior now. I got a little boy. Same name. But I'm a senior and he's a junior."

His whole face lit up then. I knew I had his ear then.

"Some nights when I don't think I can make it up over that mountain, I stay at Mizz Peele's," I said. "I hate like hell to do it, but some nights it's gotta be done. It was a helluva lot easier before the kid come. Took chances. Did what I wanted, when I wanted, *who* I wanted. This one, that one.

"Now when I go away, all I can see is that boy-a-mine's face and hear him callin' my name, and I wanna get back home as fast as I can."

Nodded. Seemed to understand.

"But sometimes, well, it ain't the smartest thing to do," I said. "The weather in his parta the country can turn nasty right quick."

"I see that," he says. "Pretty damn cole."

"Gets a damn sight worse'n this," I said, "and it's the damndest thing. Whole state might have sunshine, but it'll be snowin' from here to Cumberland. And you gotta sleep. I don't like to be on the road when I'm too tard. You gotta use your head, Phillip."

"I ain't no Phillip," he says. "My name is *Fee*-lix!"

God Almighty, I got the man's name wrong.

"Well, Felix it is then. Felix," I said, "that ain't a name you hear every doggone day."

"Well," he says, smilin', "Felicissimo, then. How's that?"

"Think I better stick with Felix," I said.

"I think so too," he says. "You know whatchew say about use your head?"

"That's the way I believe, Felix." I wanda try his name out.

"That part there is true," he says. I waited, but he didn't say no more.

"Where's your family?" I said. "Wuddia doin' in this necka the woods?"

"They're on the other side," he said. "Mama and Daddy, dead and gone. The other, well, that's a long story."

"We got us a little ways to go," I said.

Looks over, smiles. "You're too anxious," he says. "Some other time I'll tell you."

I let him be. He had his chin back down on his grip, thinkin', I reckon. I know better'n to bother a man when he's thinkin'. I know how that can be.

Hargrove

Me and Levi, we jest come inside and I'm still shakin' off the cole when Mizz Peele motions for us to wipe our feets off like she does every afternoon jest about.

He was there then. The new man, the stranger. Set at the kitchen table wid Mister Charles. Mizz Peele has the floh.

"I won't rent to couples," Mizz Peele says, not to me, not to Levi, or even Mister Charles and the stranger, but to the air, how she does. "Noddny more. No more rough-and-tumble trade under this roof. No indeedy. There's other houses for that kind of carryin's-on if that's what people have on their minds. I run a nice Christian home, like my mama did, and I aim to keep it that way."

She didn't stop till we stuck our heads in the doh. She could go on forever, that woman.

"Hargrove and Levi," she says, "come and say hello to Mister Felix. Mister Felix has come to stay with us for a spell."

We no sooner said our hellos and she was back at it.

"My mother if she was well wouldn't stand for it. I know she would think my way. Never was one to tolerate shenanigans. *And these boys!*"

Me and Levi, she meant. Gives us a cookie and tells us to share.

"Black as coal," she tells the new man. "You won't see many of their kind around here. If they had been lucky enough to have folks who care, who knows where they'd be? Oh, Mister Felix, they're as much a part of my burden as my poor mother. Every bit as much."

Woman don't even stop for air. Says:

"So you see why I must run a Christian home. To prevent the devil and all his evil ways from entering their imprayshionable heads. They'll come soon enough, such thoughts. Time enough for the devil to try and sew his evil seeds. Time for that's too close, you ask me. Time for that is just around the bend."

She was talkin' up a storm about us all right. Her idea of us. Stood at the stove, talkin' and stirrin' the big kettle. Talk and stir, talk and stir; mostly talk.

"That Myrtle and her Floyd," she says, still stirrin', "how they used to keep me up at nights!"

Me and Levi, like we attached to some machine, puts our hands up to cover our faces, to hide the laughin'. Ole Henrietta don't like nobody laughin' when she talks. Claims it's a sign of disrespect and if she catches you, she'll clip you one behind the ears, jest hard enough to letch you know she's there and she don't like it none.

I looked over at the stranger and he got his hand over his mouth, and *he's* shakin' from side to side. Man better learn to look serious. I look serious, but I ain't. Got plenty practice wid that white woman.

Maybe she seen him try and hide it. I couldn't say. I don't rightly know. I do know she put him to work right away. Oh, she did him the courtesy of lettin' come to supper. Even Mizz Caledonia got a chance to set down to supper wid the rest of us.

(Me and Levi, we got our own table.)

But right after he et and said "Thank you for the sawreech, ma'am," and durn if I know what kinda talk that is, the new boarder got a job to do. She had him sweep the floh right after he et. No time to lose, I guess she figgered. That's how that woman is: *I* know.

The new man, he a hard one to figger. Good clothes, dress clothes on his back and the same time he gotta sweep the floh and take out the gubbage. Clothes're duhty from walkin' 'em roads. (She says she'll clean 'em for him, and you can bet cash money she will: Mizz Henrietta Peele a woman of her word. *She'd* be better if she had somebody who'd do sumpn 'sides listen to her go on like she does, but I ain't seen no takers for the job. How long she been widout a man is anybody's guess. Me and Levi, we give up guessin'.)

Got rough hands, the new man. Maybe he a fighter or somebody who got his hands cut up an uncommon lot. He ain't uncommonly big, but he a strong so-and-so. Saw him sweep wid one hand and pick up the table, that good mahogany table, and you know how heavy that is, belongs to Mizz Caledonia, like everything else here, not ole Henrietta, with jest one hand. *One hand.*

Done lost a finger or most of it. Got what they call a nub. Maybe he lost it fightin' on the roads or sumpn. Maybe he hurt somebody real bad and they did that to him and he did sumpn else and now he spends all his time on the roads.

He got the looks, I give him that. Ain't like me and Levi, but he a little on the dark side. Can't think of his name, but he puts you in the minda him. It'll come to me.

Talks durn funny talk. Like Southern folk but wid some kinda accent. Wonder where he come from.

Wonder jest what kinda work he do too. He jest looking for work, he says, set there at the kitchen table. Gonna try the packinghouse. He calls it a cannery, but people around here calls it a packinghouse.

Get him a packinghouse mama first payday, I betcha.

He a quiet somebody too. Polite as pie.

I told Levi, I'll be keepin' my eye on this one.

Levi

Hargrove don't miss a beat. "How you doin' tonight, Mister Felix? Shine, Mister Felix? Anything you need, you come see Hargrove." Sweetest black boy this side of the Pacifistic Ocean.

That nigger.

That's how he does. The man no sooner off the road wid Mister Charles and that's how he does. Man's got his own troubles. One lookidum'll tellya that. But Hargrove only sees the man's dress clothes and he don't miss a beat. That boy smells money. He only needs a whiff, that boy. His nose works daytime, nighttime, allatime.

The new man, Mister Felix, wise to him already. Smiles back at Hargrove and says, "Doan bleeve so, Meester Hargrove. But if I think of anything a young boy can do, and I ain't able, I'll letch you know."

That takes ole Hargrove down a notch or two. Goes back to his milk. But he started sumpn.

"Boy," the new man says, "tell me some. Why you stick your nose in the glass to drink that cow juice?"

Ole Hargrove, smart as he thinks he is, ain't got no comeback. He ain't smart enough. Don't know enough to smile.

And he calls me Dumbhead. Dumbhead and Caruso. Tells me, "If you couldn't carry a tune, Levi, you'd be a nincompoop." Don't know what that means, but it don't sound good.

I never say nothin' back. He's thirteen, I'm nine. But I kin do sumpn he cain't. Heard white folk say I got a gift.

"So what you think about the new man comes here in good dress clothes?" I ask him outside after supper.

Hargrove takes his time to answer. His mind is somewheres else. He's got a rubber ball he likes to throw against the house, sumpn he ain't sposta do. He kin throw against the barn, not the house. Fancies hisself a pitcher. A lefty. I don't know how he does it. So dark out I cain't hardly see.

"Give ole Henrietta somebody to tell her troubles," he says between pitches. "She'll be givin' him an earful about us, if she ain't already. The others too. Woman don't spare nobody."

"What's his story?" I ask Hargrove. They all got stories: only too glad to tell 'em.

"Don't know chet," Hargrove says. "Man don't talk much. Leas' that's how he started out. Might not be able to get a word in edgewise tomorra. I my-self am keepin' an eye on him."

Yeah, smart boy, but he done seen you comin'.

(Thought it. Didn't say it.)

"Hargrove!" Mizz Henrietta. *"Put that ball down and come inside. You too, Levi. I know you're out there."*

Henrietta

She is my mother and my responsibility. Don't think I don't know that. Don't think that for one minute. I know that as well as I know the back of my hand. I tell myself every morning and every night: *It is my lot in life. Everyone has their burden. She is mine.* Like Daddy, before he died. It's the cards I drew. It's just the way Bradford Munson told me that time. Told me and never came back to see me. Never even passed this way again. He wasn't right to carry on with me the way he did and then go and do me that way.

But what he said, he was oh so right about that.

He wasn't the only one; there were others. Quite a few others if I stop and think and count up. Men boarders, gentlemen callers. Quite a few over the years. I've never stopped to count up. Telling me, asking me why I don't put her in a home. A Christian home, they call it. Even a Catholic home. Let the nuns take care of her.

Because I have no life of my own. This is no life. You can't call this any kind of a life.

Every morning, it is the same: lying here, waiting for the day to begin. For my life to start. My day begins and ends with her. It ain't right. Feeding her and washing her and making sure all hours of the day and night that she is clean and cared for. It is my duty, by God, I know that as well as I know anything.

But when in the name of a merciful God does it end? Seems like it has been this way forever.

I had to keep her here, on this floor. It's out of necessity. People do not understand. She could not be left alone downstairs the way she is now. Once, a long time ago, she could; not now. There's no way now. She could throw a fit. Have a conniption. Make a spectacle of herself in front of these boarders. And they wouldn't stand for it. If only she had her good mind she would realize. But I know it as well as I know anything.

They've been ever so tolerant of what noise they hear. That's because they're out during the day. (And because I've looked the other way many's a time, at night.) So they don't get to hear the worst of it. She saves that for me. The worst of it comes in the daytime when they're out of the house and she is alone with me. That's when she shows herself. That's when her worst side comes out.

I know how she does. I've seen her play-act with the boarders often enough. Last night, with the new man, she was on her best behavior. Always is, when it's somebody new. What she tells them when she gets the chance, God only knows. If she ever went on at night the way she does here alone with me in the day, why, these boarders would have the screaming meemies a match for anything she's liable to pull.

Lord have mercy. Those boarders would be gone before you could say Jack Rabbit. Surely they would and you couldn't blame them. Not one bit. And if I was to leave her downstairs, untied, it would happen right quick. Because she's gotten so much worse, you see. And if I took the hankie out of her mouth, what would she say?

I know the answer to that all too well.

More lies. Just like the last time. Shamed me, made me feel ashamed, the last time I thought I was doing a righteous, caring deed. But then, oh, God, forgive her soul, the lies she told. My own mother: a liar. Mama was, is, and always will be a liar when it comes to me.

Liar, liar, pants on fire. She will tell no more tales about me in this house.

Oh. There it is. Her cane hitting the bare hardwood floor. Louder than usual this morning. She must have to shoo-shoo. Yes, my call to arms. My day has begun.

"Coming, Mama. Be right there. I'm coming."

I tried with the new man, last night. I tried to tell him of my burden. Seems like an altogether nice man. Very quiet and nice and some kind of foreigner. Foreigners from foreign lands. They always seem to know something we don't.

I hope and pray he will be the one to understand me in a way the others do not, cannot. I cannot seem to make people understand my burden to save my soul.

Caledonia

On my solemn promise not to disturb anyone, I was allowed
to go down the stairs last night and sit to supper with the others.
That's when I saw the new boarder for the first time. Man made
me laugh.

Henrietta told him who I was. Ashamed of me as always but
knowing she faced even more shame if she didn't. The others,
they knew me; but the new boarder never saw me before, so I
needed explaining. Heard of me before surely, of that I have no
doubt, but never saw me before.

I said "Howjadew" and he said "Hello, ma'am," ever so
politely. *And so handsome!* By far the most handsome gentleman
we've taken in since we've been takin' people in. Much handsomer
than that actor we had a few years back.

Henrietta introduced us. His name is Felix.

He said to me, "Caledonia? What kinda name is that?"

I told him, laughing I was, for the first time in a month of
Sundays, "Landsakes, it's just a name, like any other."

"Now that's where you're wrong," he says. *"That's your name!"*

I told the gentleman, I *knew* he was a foreigner, not just because of his looks but he had manners, stood up when I came into the room while all the others sat, that my father named me.

He was from Scotland, my father, I told the gentleman.

"Oh, I see. A Scotchman," he says.

"No," I said, laughing, "a *Scots*man."

"Now I gotchew," he says, silly thing.

Mister Felix said he came from It'ly. I told him I'd heard of It'ly but had never been there.

He told me that in the Eyetalian language, his name meant happiest, and he was the happiest one. He said his name for me, but I could never say it for love nor money.

Well, I can see he is a happy-go-lucky gentleman. Very pleasant to talk to, and handsome, as I said.

Most of the other boarders don't speak unless they're spoken to, and they don't wish to be spoken to. They have their ways of letting you know. As a rule they never speak to me, even when I go down the stairs and sit quietly in the sitting room with those boys, Levi and Hargrove, or when Henrietta lets me sit at the supper table, not so much as even a polite inquiry into my health which Henrietta says is failing.

When Henrietta went to take me upstairs last night, Mister Felix said "Pleasant dreams" and I said "Same to you."

I am going to try and be nice and quiet today and not disturb Henrietta in any way so that maybe she will let me go down to supper tonight and I can see the nice gentleman again and feed myself.

Oh, I wish I didn't, but I do have to make water.

Felicissimo

That ole lady there, she's all right. Lot more fun that her big little daughter, I'll tellya right now.

The daughter, she's the cat's meow, she is. We all gotta get along in this world and it takes all kinds, but that woman, she takes the cake, I doan mean maybe.

Set there at the supper table she gave me her whole life story. *First night.* The other boarders set there, eat, she din care. I din say much. Doan pay, I found out a long time ago. But liss to her talk, I doan think that woman ever went with a man in her life. She ain't no spring chicken, either.

Talk about her mother, the ole lady, set right there at the table like she was some stranger. Oh the daughter, she did this, she did that. Talk like she been take care of her mother *for years.* Which come to find out ain't been two years if that long, one ole-timer there tole me.

Not very long and if you ask me, the ole lady's better in the head than the daughter. By a long shot, brother. Walked slow, with a cane, to come down the stairs. Then, seemed outa thin air, the daughter was tie the ole lady's hands with rope. Set't the table. Never saw anything like that before in ma life. I couldn bleeve.

I said to Henrietta, the daughter, I said't just for de'lment, "Why you keep this young lady prisoner? Is she wand by the law?"

Old lady was set there, liss.

I said't, just cut up and fool, but I'll be frank with you: Hungry as I was, din seem right to me to set't the table with a plate fulla food and that ole lady set next to me with her hands and now I notice her feet too all tie up with ropes.

Was think to maself, Whattadahell do you call that? Wasn any damn business a-mine, wasn ma mother, *but still*.

The daughter, I could tell she din like very well what I was say, but she finely loose up the rope so her mother could feed herself. The ole lady did all right to eat. Lookt to me like she was starve.

I was pretty damn hungry maself, so I got busy, but I was watch her. She was no more than skin and bones.

I doan know what was cause it, but oh man, all of a sudden the daughter, she starda talk. Once she starda talk she wouldn shut up. I had et ma supper, had apple pie and a shoop of ice cream for dessert and two cupsa coffee and she still hadn shut up. Was almost sorry I spoke up.

But't hadda be done.

After the others got up from the table, she said to me, "Ma mother is not right in the head." I thought to maself, And you are? "She could be a harm to herself and others. The way she gets to carryin'-on, I wonder sometimes how I can take it. You know, Mister Felix, a body can only take so much."

I wanda say, "What do you have to take, sister? She's your mother, ain't she?" But I din say a damn thing. I wanda say, "This ole lady seems all right to me." But she stard up again. I swear, you couldn shut that woman up if you poured a pisspot over her head.

I winkt to the ole lady, and what did she do but wink back to me. All this time her daughter was talk a blue streak, and I wanda say, "Will you please shut up?"

But I was a guest in the house, you know, first night, and I needt a place to stay and a job too for that matter. I din need no more trouble than I already was in.

All right. I was liss while she was tell all. When she was all in, I took a chance.

I said, half joke, "This young lady here looks pretty calm now. She looks like the kinda girl can behave herself. Why doan you take the rope off her feet and be done with it?"

Well, the ole lady, she *laughed.* You couldn hear her, but she had a smile you need a rule to measure. She lookt to me, I lookt to her, like two kids.

Good thing the daughter's back was turned. But justthatquick the daughter swung around, and the ole lady, she lookt downta floor. The daughter, she din know *what* to make of it.

While she was look for some else to say, I notice some: The daughter was a good-size woman. Not fat, but not small by a long shot. The ole lady was a little thing, not much more than skin and bones. Still, a pretty woman. I liked to see her smile. I got a big keek watch her.

Finely the daughter says to her mother, "All right, Mama. I'll leave these ropes off you for a little while. But you got to promise me one thing," and the ole lady's eyes got so big. The daughter tole her mother, "You have to promise me you'll behave yourself tonight. Mister Felix is brand-new here, and we don't want him to see your ugly side, do we, Mama?"

That's the Christ's truth. That's how she spoke to her mother, her own flesh and blood. Sorprise me the ole lady din haul off and bop her one first chance come along.

I never saw anything like that in ma life. Ropes on your own mother. And the ole lady, she din do a damn thing, just set there, mind her own business. Spoke to me, a few words here, a few words there. Din get a chance to say much. Her big little daughter was the talker in that house. That was plain to see.

But the ole lady and I, we had her goats up for a minutes or two. The ole lady's a pistol, no question about't. She's somebody I bleeve I could have a swell time with.

Set there, at least she din have them damn ropes all over her like she was no better than a prisoner in her own home.

Up in the loft, I reckon, that din last long.

Epp

He's sitting outside the office when I come in. Looks up, smiles. Reminds me of some Broadway character. All dressed up in his Sunday suit. Dressed better than I am. Even sits like a gen'leman.

First I think he's from the government. But those fellas don't even give me the courtesy any more. They walk in like they own the place. Then I think he's from the New York office, here to take my place. But, I think again, if that's the case, he'd probably be sitting *in* my office, not out there in the hallway.

I don't know what he is.

Preacher. Snake oil salesman. Somebody wants work.

Today's Thursday. Usually they're in here bright and early every Monday. Not many want a job bad enough they're in here before I am, like this fella. Everybody needs a job Monday. Come Friday, they get their pay, and that's the end of it. Till the next time. Couple weeks go by they're back in here and it's the same old story all over again.

I've never seen this one before. I'd remember him if I had.

I ask Rosalie to go out and see what he wants.

She comes back and says, "Work. Man says he'll take anything you've got. He'll even sweep the floors, if that's all you have. He's no floor sweeper, Myron."

Rosalie my darling. Last night I jumped her and she still ain't over it. Never fails. Every time I do, she starts taking liberties. You cannot mix business with pleasure but never.

(But what can you do? It's a long way from New York, and this little Irish girl likes it even if it's a circumcised Jew from Brooklyn old enough to be her fatha she gets it from.)

"Have him fill out the application and check back on Monday," I tell her. The standard line.

She's back before you can say one-two-three.

"Says he'd like to meet you. In case something comes along. Says he's not a packer."

"What is he if he ain't a packer? A doctor of psychology?" Sometimes you gotta talk to her that way. Rosalie my darling.

"He says he's a machinist."

"Oh, a machinist, is he?"

"I'm only telling you what he said, Myron. Fixing canning machines is his line. Says he has letters from different ones he's worked for."

Points her little ass at me. Usually she says they're clean and that they swear up and down they never touch the stuff, not even on Saturday night.

"Didn't you tell him we already have a mechanic?"

"We do?" she says. "Who's that?"

"Johnny Johnson is our mechanic, Rosalie, and you know it." She hates Johnny Johnson. I don't know why, but I can guess.

"The man outside is a *machinist*, Myron."

"Mechanic, machinist, it's all the same," I tell her.

"Pooch is a good-for-nothing, Myron." That's what they all call him. "I've heard you say as much yourself."

Rosalie. One day I'm gonna jump her right in the middle of lunch hour. Lock the door and put her on the desk. Or maybe I'll wait a day when the U.S. government is here. *And leave the door wide open.* Give the federal boys something to see. Won't J. Edgar be pleased? And New York?

"Trust me," she says, "this one won't be back, Myron. He's not from around here. Passing through, looking, that's what he's doing. You let this one go, you might regret it."

"All right, all right. Bring him in. It don't cost me to talk to nobody."

"Myron, you could use a dependable man."

"Thanks for telling me my business, Rosalie."

She smiles. Sweetest damn smile. Smile to break your heart.

He comes in behind her. Keeps his eyes down, off her keister, which tells me he has real willpower, while she does the introducing.

A gen'leman, when the time comes he looks me right in the eye. Firm handshake. Rosalie, she can't keep her eyes off him, even after last night. He's no kid, but lucky for me, he ain't giving her the time of day. He's a damn good-looking fella, no two ways about it, and dressed even better than I took notice, out there by Rosalie.

Rosalie hands me his application. Fancy handwriting. He's an Italian. Could almost pass for a Jew. Too dark, though. No wonder Rosalie couldn't say his last name.

Almost like he could read my mind, he says to me, "Is your name Epp, or Eppstein?"

"Eppstein." It's out before I know it. Not even New York knows my last name. Or bothers to ask. "I shortened it."

"Well," he says, "what's in a name?"

"This way," I said, "it's easier for people to say."

Smiles. He's a happy-go-lucky sort. He wouldn't care what my name was if it was printed on my forehead.

Says with a poker face, "My father was Jewish."

Get him. He's a kidder. So we both had a laugh.

"Rosalie," I tell her because she's already seen and heard enough for one day, "go take a look-see what's doing out there." She ain't too happy about it, but she goes.

I told the man, "Rosalie's my eyes and ears out there on the floor." He can take that any way he wants. But he just nods, smiles. Reminds me of somebody deef and dumb, but he ain't neither.

I look over his papers. He's been in Boulder, Colorado; Bridgeport, Connecticut; Indianapolis; St. Louis. The last place was Cincinnati. He's forty-two years of age. (Looks twenty-five.) Left the country. Came back in -twenty-two.

"I see here you're an experienced man, Mister —" He had to say his name for me.

"Oh," he says, "you betcher life."

I asked him, "Why didn't you stay in New York or Jersey when you got off the boat? Stay around your own people? People that talk the same language. That's what my people did."

"'Cause," he says, "I din want to." *Because he didn't want to.* "I wand some diff'rent." Not a bit afraid to speak up.

"How did you come by your first job," I said, "way out there in Boulder, Colorado? Tell me that."

"Wunna ma brothers," he says, "he was a big boss out there at the time. Gave me the job. Sweep the floors, to start. Ten cents a day."

"What did you do with yourself? To pass the time?"

"Oh, I went to the school at night. Learn to speak Engleesh."

"I mean for fun," I said, "for pleasure."

"Oh," he says, "go to the picture show two-three times a week." I thought he'd just stepped out of one. "Cost me five cents, at one time. Them days are gone bye-bye."

"You seen a lotta country," I said. "Any reason for that?"

Them clothes, he could be a gangster. A man on the lam. But this fella, if somebody was to stick a gun in his belly, he'd tell 'em where to stick it. Lothario was more like it, with a string of broken hearts left behind. Me, I don't care. As long as he don't try to make time with Rosalie my darling.

Finally he says, "I wanda see for maself."

I swear it. That's what the man said.

Talks as slow as some of the ones from around here.

"You have a drinking problem, any such thing as that?" I ask him. "Better you tell me now if you do. What I'm getting at, is, can you hold a steady job? Are you a good, reliable man?"

Says to me, "You can see right there, cange you? That'll tell you the whole story better than I can. I work two-three years one place, two-three years someplace else. Left when I was ready, no sooner. Always try to better maself. Never was fired from a job in ma life. To answer your question."

Talks so slow. Says just what he means. Smiles. I don't know what the hell he is, but *he* knows what he is. No one better tell him different, neither. Skinny, though. He's out at Henrietta Peele's place. She'll fatten him up. She should take some of hers and give it to him. She's got some to spare.

Without so much as a knock, Rosalie pushes open the door. That's not like her. She's breathing like last night.

"Myron, you better come quick. There's beans all over the floor, and Johnson's nowhere to be found. I shut down the line and told Rufus to go look for him."

"Good girl, Rosalie. You did the right thing, only Rufus won't know where to look. You just calm yourself."

The man speaks up. "Doan get excited. That doan do no good."

I don't know what came over her; but she changed, caught her breath, I guess.

It's only eight-thirty. I'll be damn if I'm gonna lose a whole day's work because Johnny Johnson's off on a toot. Which has happened before.

So I said, "All right, Felix. Let's see what you can do, young man."

Rosalie gets him a work uniform he can put over his dress clothes. There ain't much I can do about his shoes. Don't seem to bother him. He's smiling, ready to go.

"Follow me," I said, "I'll take you out on the floor."

Afterwards, I look around for Johnson. He is my mechanic, after all. But he's nowhere on the premises, so I send Neptune out to look. Ten-thirty, nothing. Eleven-thirty, still nothing. Noon, thereabouts, he shows up on the floor. Stinking.

When I fired him, there in the office, he told me, "You're a damn dirty Jew, Epp."

"Cleaner than you'll ever be," I said. And I told him, I said, "It's *Mister* Eppstein to you, *Pooch.*"

Felicissimo

I got a job today.

Yeah boy, first fool day in town and I got a job. Sorprise the daylights outa me. 'Cause I wasn expect that. Hope for the best, but that's all you can do.

Jew fellow there is the big boss. Seemt to be a pretty good skate. Seemt to me. This morning when I went to see him, he had his hands full. Man oh man, he had trouble. They had a mechanic, but he was off some damn place, nobody knew where.

Girl, a friendly somebody, came back from the floor and she tole the big boss, this Jew fellow, Zo-and-Zo's not here.

Next thing you know the big boss lookt to me and said, "Felix, let's see what you can do. Do you think you can fix the machine?" I tole him, "I'll do ma best," and the next thing you know the girl was put the work yuniform — a big apron was all it was — over me.

I went out where they work and they had beans *all over* the damn floor I doan mean maybe. Just gonta waste. Made me sick to ma stomach to see. If you was ever hungry you know what I mean.

I know the machine, they call it a Max-Am, as good as the backa ma hand. Better. I saw the big boss was plen-tee worried, so to put his mind to rest, I tole him, "Just a minute and I'll tellya what I'm gonna do." I did too.

There was a young fellow there, set his backside down on a crate. He was just set there, half asleep, so I ask the big boss, "How 'bout that young man there? Can he lend me a hand?"

Big boss said, "Sure. *Billy!*" and Billy woke up then. "Lend Mister Felix a hand." He did.

Meantime, they sent a color man out to find the master *mécanique*. Where the devil he was, nobody knew. Everybody was hush up.

Two, three hours pass by and still no master *mécanique*.

We work and we work, just me and this young boy. He hand me a wrench, a screwdriver, whatever I was need. Hold the light. Ask me diff'rent questions. Saved me many a step, and when the job was done, I tole him I was appreciate all he done. I said thank you and reach in ma pocket and took out a quarter. *He was smile then.* When he was go off to lunch, he was *whistle*.

I got a big keek watch him. Just a boy.

I happ to glance at ma watch, and it was ten minutes to twelve. Noontime. So we had the job done by noontime. The line was ready for business right after lunch.

Oh, the big boss he couldn get over. "Oh, Felix," he said to me, "how did you do it?" He was in a bad way and he knew and I knew.

I tole the big boss just what I done. I adjust this one and I adjust that one, but he was need new parts bad and this wasn gonna last forever.

Took me back to his office. "You tend to it," he said. "Fifty dollars a week. Begin today."

We shook hands and out I went. Was feel pretty damn good.

Little later Zo-and-Zo, the mechanic, came back from wherever he was. I doan think the color man ever did find him; he just came back on his own when he felt like.

I heard the big boss call him Johnson. "Step in ma office," he tole this Johnson.

Johnny Johnson, that was his name. Redhead like Red. Has the freckles all over his face. Look to me like he had the measles. Big man, but he din look like he was in too gooda shape. Was sway back and forth, to walk. Face *so red*. Was drunk all right.

They went to the office where I was this morning and everybody could hear. The big boss tole Johnson, "Some man off the street came in here today and did the job I pay you damn good money to do. You're gone, nobody can find you. Time after time, but this is the last time."

Johnny din say one word. Not even boo.

All the girls set outside the office there to eat they lunch. All quiet as church mice. *Shhh. Shhh.* They doan want nobody talk so they can hear Johnny get chew out. So they all heard the big boss tell Johnny he din have no more job.

Johnny said some then, but I din understand what was. *Slam* the door behind him, sorprise me the glass din break.

After he came out he din do a damn thing but pull down his breeches, the girls set there eat they lunch, and take a leak.

All you could hear was the pee splash against the wall there.

Then what did he do but turn around to the girls, show them what he had. Like they never saw before. Took seemt like forever to pull up his breeches. Then out he went, still sway this way and that way. Din say a word to nobody.

Oh boy. Then the girls starda talk to one another. Jabber-jabber-jabber. Remind me of chickens. I guess nobody felt no more like eat.

I felt sorry but wasn ma fault. I din think too mucha what he done, but I mind ma own affairs. I din tell that fellow to go out there and get cockeyed drunk one eye can't see the other. Somebody tole me it wasn the first time he done that kinda monkey business, and the big boss, the Jew, wouldn stand for it no more.

I doan know why people do the things, I swear I doan.

'Cause when the whistle blew at five o'clock, quit time, Johnny was back again. This time worse than before. He lookt to me and I lookt to him and I thought to maself, Brother, you wanna fight, come and get't.

He was look here, look there. Look all around. But din say boo to me and I never said one word to him. Course I doan look for trouble. Never did for that concern. I wasn cause him to lose his job. I din blow on him. He did hisself.

(Was remind me of ma brother Mike, that way. Same damn foolishness.)

Lookt and lookt but come to find out I doan think he was look for me. Who he was look for, I doan know. I left.

Walk to the boardinghouse, I starda think. Oh, diff'rent things. Struck me funny, those girls there. They let the line run till the boss's secretary, she shut it down. They knew better. They knew some was wrong. *Had to.* But no, they stood there, watch all those beans fall on the floor, go to waste.

Some of them doan know their front side from their backside, you ask me. But they think they pretty damn smart. Act like they are. Ask them a question, can be any damn thing, and they got a smart answer for you every time. Think they can make a fool outa anybody comes along can't talk as good as they can. Like they can do so good.

All right. When I'm soft I'm hard, and when I'm hard I'm soft.

Some people ain't got no sense. All they care about is that damn clock on the wall and if the big boss, Mister Epp, *Eppstein*, is watch. He was need eyes in the backa his head to keep up with some of them, I ain't kid you. Saw for maself what he was up against.

Some damn funny people in this world.

While that boy and I was work, they was set on their backside and ask me questions. Thought't was funny, to begin, but after a while they got on ma nerves so damn bad I was wish they'd shut up.

"What's your name?" Then when I tole 'em, they said to me, "*Fee*-lix, that's a nice name. Like Felix the Cat! . . . Take your time, *Fee*-lix. We ain't in no hurry to get back to work. ... Take your time, take your time. The pusher is out today. ... Talk to us, *Fee*-lix. ... Say, ain't you cute!"

Play along as best as I could. You got to in this world. The ole women and the young girls, they ain't so bad. (I see they got some young girls work can't be more than fifteen. If that. Little toots. Pretty as a picture but too young for me.) It's the ones in between act so damn smart.

While I was at work, somebody, I got a pretty good idea who was, din do a damn thing but come along and goose me.

Cackle-cackle-cackle. You was think you was in a henhouse. They thought that was so funny they couldn stop from laugh. Made me mad, but I din let on. I had no time for such foolishness 'cause I had a job to do, only that boy there to help me.

But next time. Next time whoever was mi' get the sorprise of their life, you watch and see.

I doan know why people think they haveta act smart, I really doan. Never did. I like to have fun: just talk, cut up and fool. Doan mean a damn thing by it. You haveta have some fun or else this world doan mount to much. But not at the other people's expenses.

That's how I feel about't.

So anyway — you know anyway? — I got a job today.

Hoo-*ray*.

You have a job in this country, and oh man, you're a king!

Levi

Well, well, *well.*

Everybody so doggone smart in this necka the woods and here comes this Eyetalian fella and first real workin' day comes along and he goes and gits hisself a job jestlikethat. *Hah!*

Everybody settin' up and takin' notice. It ain't jest any ole job neither. Mister Felix, he's a master mechanic. Tole me so hisself.

But I was a way aheada everybody. I figgered it thataway. 'Causea them hands.

Even so. That Felicissimo — Mister Felix, we calls him — don't put on no airs. He come back from workin' all day at the packinghouse a pleasant somebody.

Wondered to my-self if he'd have that big smile ifften he didn't find work today.

I dunno. He was smilin' when I first seen him set at the table wid Mister Charles. I think he come in the doh smilin'.

Parta me thinks there ain't nothin' kin hold this new man down.

Don't talk big nor show off none.

Jest handles hisself like he knows sumpn the next fella don't.

Or forgot.

Or else maybe ain't caught onto chet.

Hargrove

I seen it first thing walkin' back from where Levi and me we go to school. Not the rayglar school, but our little shack, to the side. No sooner out the doh and I seen it. Long ways away.

Levi singin' so low like he does don't pay it no mind. He's one boy who kin only handle one idea in his head at a time. More than one confounds him.

So Levi, he don't see it. I don't expect him to. I reckon he's got the voice, but he ain't got the eye like ole Hargrove.

Long ways away I kin tell by the embellum — that ram on the front — it's a Dodge.

Sleek machine. Don't draw stares like a Ford or even a Pontiac will, 'specially 'round these parts. It ain't new, but it ain't so ole neither. Looks to me like maybe a -thirty-two. Two dohs. Got a tar on the side. Right sporty.

I knowed right away whose it was. Don't take a ton of bricks to fall on ole Hargrove.

The new man. The foreigner. It's hisn.

It figgered. Couldn't be nobody else. He only been here a month or so, but he look lost, like a man widout a car will look if he evah had one. Had that look about hisself.

I whistled when I seen it.

"You don't even know the tune," Levi says, coming back from wherevah he was.

"The machine," I tell him, "look at the machine!"

"So?" he says. *So.*

So there he was, the new man. Got a rag in his hand. Goin' to town wid it. Good afternoon for it. Sunny. We start to get some nice days now. He musta got off work early to go and get it. Shinin' it up real nice. Makin' a nice job of it. Smokin' his big see-gar.

Shine. Sweat. Smile. Smoke. Shine some more. Never loses his smile. Has fun even to work.

Nobody has cars at the house, 'cept Mizz Peele and ole Henrietta. They got two cars in the carriage house. One a real ole Ford, the other a right nice Buick. Never run 'em since I been here. Tars look like they start to rot.

"Zat yours?" I ask him. I ain't bashful.

"You betcher life," he says. "How do you like it, Meester Hargrove? You, Meester Levi?"

"It's a right sporty machine," I tell him. I'm thinkin', How kin he do it? The others cain't and he kin. How? Some master mechanic. I guess ole Pooch Johnson mida had a car too iffen he didn't like his hooch so much. Mida had a job too. Still drinkin', job or no job, last I heard.

Levi's got his hand on the embellum.

"Doan put your fingers all over ma new car," the new man says. He ain't jokin' none, this time.

Levi gets his feelin's hurt over nothin'. Takes his hand away like it was scalded. Won't even look up. New man sees it.

Says, "I'll tellya what I'll do with you boys." He stops shine. Still smile, smoke and sweat. "*If* you're good boys and do like I tell you, I'll take you for a spin. How's that?"

"We're good boys," I tell him before Levi has a chance to put his foot in it. "Ain't we good boys, Levi?"

Levi nods. Don't talk much when his feelin's is hurt.

"Now, then," the new man says and tosses a rag my way, another to Levi. "Shine her up real good now, and off we go."

I get to it, but Levi, he jest stands there.

"Hurry up," Mister Felix tells him, "'cause we wait on you."

Levi kin be Mister Slow Motion unless he gets a notion to move.

"Shake it up," Mister Felix tells him, "we ain't got all day."

Levi shinin' the big ram now like nobody's bidness.

"Okay," Mister Felix says after a spell, "that's look good. Let's went."

A crazy Eyetalian man and two colored boys ride around on a warm, almost spring day. I ain't thinkin' what ole Henrietta will say. I know she will have a lot to say. I don't care. I'm too busy thinkin' which big white boys and they pretty girlfriends will be on the road and see us in this -thirty-two Dodge coo-pay wid an Eyetalian man smoke his beeg see-gar in the front seat drivin' me and Levi in the back seat like he was work for us.

That's a pitcher.

Charles

It's a -thirty-two Dodge DK Eight. A two-door coo-pay.

Fee behind the wheel, don't you know. Them colored boys, Hargrove and Levi, along for the ride. Fee's treat, I reckon. Likes kids, Fee. Somebody to be silly with.

Fee smokin' his big see-gar. His trademark. Still in his work clothes, it looks like.

Right snazzy for a Dodge. It ain't no Pontiac nor one of your Fords. Not nearly as much get-up-and-go. Hell, they have Fords around here with the cast-iron flathead V-8 motors and the front axles set the way some fellas — friends, ole boys I know — want them and in some cases need them. Them cars are so fast the revenuers can't keep up.

That Dodge is a good, reliable automobile. Decent speed. But it ain't no car for any man thinkin', playin' with the idear of racin' the law.

Course that wouldn't be Fee nohow.

A sporty machine, though, that pa'tic'lar model.

Levi

March left us a lamb, but April has come in like a hungry mountain lion so the men cain't even go outside or set on the porch after supper. They all set in the pollar where Mizz Henrietta lets 'em smoke and chew and tell they stories. Like it's still wintertime.

Mister Felix, he a see-gar smoker. Gives me and Hargrove the wrapper rings and tells us to give 'em to our best girlfriends but don't get married.

He a funny man. He a singer too.

"Fiammifero, fiammifero," he sings. That's sumpn to do wid a match. A spark. A flame. All in Eyetalian. I think he made it up. Wouldn't put it past him.

Mizz Henrietta said right off she didn't mind the singin', why even Levi, this black-as-coal boy here, is a singer. But she tole him he mus'n't sing anything that wasn't clean 'cause these here are two impray-imprayshionable niggerboys sent to her to get right, to be shown the light, and they was her Christian respon-responsibility. Went on quite serious for quite a spell.

"Yes, ma'am," Mister Felix says when she finally gets done. And no sooner than that he starts singin' "O Sole Mio" at the toppa his lungs. Everybody in the pollar, even ole Mister Himmler, smiles; and he hardly evah do. He ain't no smiler. Act like he ain't got time for it.

Mister Felix, he ain't like that. He a pleasant somebody.

I take notice Mizz Caledonia been comin' downta supper these last few weeks. Evah since the new man come. Strange how that happened at jest the same time.

Mister Felix, he a ladies' man. Knows how to talk 'em up. Even the ole lady, she takes a shine to him. He's *real* quiet. Then all of a sudden he'll come out wid sumpn. Usely silly. Like askin' me and Hargrove why we cain't keep our nose outen the glass. Like that.

Wid ole Caledonia, he asks her about her boyfriends. "Any new men come a-courtin' you to-day, young lady?" he asks her. Or he says, "Hey there, how did you get so good-lookin'?" She jest laughs. So quiet you cain't hardly hear her.

I thought she was in a bad way. Come to find out she act normal as anybody in this house when her daughter, Mizz Henrietta, takes 'em ropes offen her.

Silliest durn thing I evah seen. Hargrove, he say the same.

First night Mister Felix come here Mizz Caledonia come down, set at the table wid them ropes all ovah her he looks *so sad.* Like it was him wearin' 'em, not her. I ain't never seen nothin' like it. He didn't do nothin' but look ovah to Mizz Henrietta and say, "Is that necessary?"

They even stop chewin', settin' at the supper table there, when he come out wid it. Somebody choked on they food and had a coughin' spell.

Well no wonder.

Mizz Henrietta, you could tell she didn't like it much. You could tell she was a-minda say, "Ain't no affair of yourn, new man. You pays by the week and behaves under my roof."

But she didn't. She didn't say a word. Jest took offen them silly durn ropes.

I reckon she didn't expect nothin' like that outen a new person, and maybe she was a little ashamed.

I say *maybe.*

Big Frankie

He calls me Toots. That new man.

He is so much fun. All the women like him.

He let me take home all those busted cans of beans. Saw me and looked the other way.

He saw me smokin' on the floor, and he looked the other way. The other men, 'specially Mitchell, make me do 'em when they catch me.

The new man, he gave me a ride home in his cah. He has a cah with white wheels. It even has a cover over the steering wheel. He let me touch it.

Felt. Feels like felt. So pretty.

All the other girls are jealous, I bet.

Never once made me do him. I thought to myself, It's comin'. He's like all the rest.

But it ain't happened chet. He don't know what it means maybe, talkin' funny like he does and all. I do not know, but he is a funny man, that I do know.

"Hello, you Toots," he says and makes me laugh.

Hargrove

It's been longer'n a month. Not two but close to it. So after supper it's jest me and him, all the other gents somewheres else, when I tell him:

"I know who you are."

"Oh, go 'way, boy. Doan bother me," the man says. "Cange you see I'm busy read this newspaper?"

Don't surprise me none. "All right," I says, "but I know who you are. And you don't haveta talk to me like a nigger neither."

He ain't readin' now. Newspaper's on his lap. "Oh no?" he says, right uppity. Cross his laigs and smoke his beeg see-gar. "I beg your puddin'. What are you if you ain't a nigger?"

"Nee-*grow*," I tell him. "You try and talk jest like the rest. But you ain't like the rest, uh-uh. So you kin stop actin' like you are. 'Cause you ain't."

Raises his eyebows at that. Eyes got so beeg. Man start to worry. "Oh," the man says, "is zat so? What makes you think so, Meester Hargrove? How do you feegure?"

"'Cause," I says, "most white folk don't talk to our folk. Never to no niggerboys. Lessen they's work to do."

"Well," the man says, "I suppose I ain't a white man, then?"

"Not like any white man I evah seen," I tell him. I tell him jest what I think: "You say you're an Eyetalian man. But you ain't entirely altogether legitmate."

"Oh, is zat so?" he says. Oh, he a sly one all right.

"Zat's so," I tell him, "zat's the troof."

Leans forward in his cheer. In a cloud of smoke. Hargrove got his ear all right. Says, "Whatchewtalk, boy?"

"You know what I talk," I tell the man. "Don't you worry, Mister Felix. Your secret's safe wid me."

"I'm glad to hear," the man says, leanin' back in his cheer again. "That's good to know." I'm playin' wid him and the man, he don't even suspect.

"You and that fancy car you jest bought."

"That's a road-es-ter, ma boy."

"Ain't nobody knows much about you," I tell him, "but I knows all. You ain't gettin' nothin' past this nigger."

"Nee-*grow*," he says. Oh, he a funny man, Mister Felix. Makes me laugh even when I'm dead set against it.

"Your secret's safe wid Hargrove," I tell him.

"You doan say. I feel better now," he says, back to his uppity white ways.

"You ain't entirely altogether legitimate," I tell him again. In case he didn't hear the first time. "You go 'round in that fancy car, whatevah you wanna call it, and them good clothes and lookin' the ladies over. You got the scratch all right. But you got a secret, too, and I'm the only one knows it."

"How did you come to know it?" he says. Ole Hargrove got his goat now. "How did you get so smart?"

Oh, I got him goin' now. It's jest me and him set in the room by ourselfs still. I ain't talkin' loud. Him neither.

"I jest knows," I says. "Hargrove, he ain't as dumb as he looks or some white folk think. You don't want nobody knowin' who you really are, do you?"

"How did you know it?" he asks, puffin' on his beeg see-gar.

"Cain't give away my secrets," I tell him. "If you wants me to call you Mister Felix, that's what ole Hargrove gonna call you. I cain't say your other name, but what's it matter? You ain't who you say you are."

"Oh no? Who am I?" White man still thinks I'm kiddin' him.

"You know who you are," I says. "Your brothers musta wanted you to go away for a while. The way I figure you must be dodgin' taxes, or else you got one of them Hollywood gals in a fambly way."

He's puffin' on his beeg see-gar. "How'd you get so smart, Hargrove?"

I knew it. See, I been watchin' him. Why nobody else thought of it jest gives testimony to how dumb white folk kin be.

"Hargrove, he ain't as dumb as he looks," I tell him again. "So what brings you to this place, Mister Groucho Marx?"

He laughin' hardy. I got him. He couldn't fool me.

"I guess you know ma secret," he says, givin' up. "Ma secret's out now."

"No, it ain't out chet," I says. "Hargrove's lips is sealed. But ain't no tellin' how long they kin stay that way."

"What's it take to keep you quiet, Hargrove? You want hush money?"

"That's right," I says, "hush money." He catches on right quick when he wants. "You got it from all them pitchers you made." He ain't denyin' nothin'. "So what's it worth to ya to stay here?"

"Well, Hargrove ma friend," the man says, "you got me between a rock and a hard place. I doan have money but what I make here. Chewsee, ma money has been cut off. Oh, it's a long story. And ma savings, shuck, that's all gone bye-bye. Too many nights paint the town red, get cockeyed drunk one eye can't see the other. You know what I mean?"

"No," I tell the man, "I don't know. But I'm right sorry. Still and all I believes we kin do bidness."

"Tellya what I'll do with you," he says, "*if* you're a good boy. You and Meester Levi. If both you boys behave, I'll buy you ice cream once in a while. ... Money's tight, ma boy. Wuddia say?"

"I think I might haveta tell" is what I say.

"You mean to tell me," the man says, "you gonna blow on me?"

I hadda nod. He a cashbox. I ain't gonna let him offen the hook. Not ole Hargrove.

"Well, all right," he says. "If you gotta, you gotta. But I thought you was ma friend."

"Bidness is bidness," I tell him.

"And I thought you was ma friend," he says again. Shakin' his head.

"I'm sorry," I says, "for your trouble."

"That's all right," the man says. "I made you ma best offer. You refuse to accept't. So I guess I can't do no business with you."

"Cain't you call on your brothers? Won't they help you out? You got more'n me," I tell the man. "You got a fambly. I ain't never had a fambly. Levi, he the same. What kinda fambly won't help out one of they own when he needs help? In his hour of need?"

"You're tellin' me," he says. "That's zactly how I feel about't."

"That's some fambly you got," I says.

He shakes his head. "Doan I know," he says.

"You sleep on it," I tell him. "I ain't gonna blow on you since you in such a bad way. That ain't right. I'll even call you Mister Felix. For appearance' sake. But you and I both know, don't we?"

"To be sure," he says. "Thank you, ma friend."

"Don't thank me chet," I says. "I said sleep on it. You don't know. Relations might improve chet."

"I hope so," he says, puffin' on that beeg ole see-gar like he ain't got a care in the world. He all smiles now.

That's an actor for ya.

Levi

Mister Felix is settin' in the cheer, smokin' his big see-gar when Mizz Henrietta comes in. We done et already.

"Mister Felix," she says, "I know you dearly love our dogs. But my father always said a house is no place for a dog. And that's always been a house rule. We never allow them in the house." Mizz Henrietta talks the same way to Mister Felix as she do Hargrove and me. A growed man.

Mister Felix knows people. Makes so his eyes got real big. He kin be a silly so-and-so.

"Well I'll be doggone," he says and looks down at Queenie and Tess. "How did you two young ladies get in here? *Hey boy!* You Levi. Did you see these two young ladies in here before?"

They right under his feets.

"Not me," I say. I seen 'em when I follied him in the room.

They jest look up at him. Two sad-eyed hound bitches. Mother and daughter. They don't know what to do.

"Run along," Mizz Henrietta tells 'em, "run along. *Scat.*"

They don't listen to her. She could be talkin' to herself.

"They ole dogs," I say.

"Can't hear so good," Mister Felix says. "I notice maself."

Mizz Henrietta is all het up.

"Mister Felix," she says, *"get those dogs out of this house this minute!"* Anybody hear her might think the house was on fire.

Mister Felix don't move fast for nobody. Goes at his own speed. Takes his own sweet time. Says it don't do no good to rush a thing. I think the same.

Finally he tells the dogs sumpn in Eyetalian and they put they paws on his lap and they faces next to hisn. "No kisses," he tells 'em, but they do as they please. He gets up then and they folly him outen the room like they know Eyetalian as good as him.

I hear the back doh shut. The dogs is out now. Mizz Henrietta is still in the smoke room. It ain't over chet. She act like she forgot I am still there. Where I ain't sposta be nohow.

Taps her foot. Acts like everybody on her time.

Mister Felix comes back in his own sweet time. Hums a tune. We both like music.

"Funny damn weather," he says. "Turn so cole you freeze your backside off."

"Now Mister Felix," she says, "there's no call for that kind of talk in the house. And the weather, you have to expect that. In this part of the country."

"Excuse me, ma'am," he says. "But when I come in for supper, I thought to maself, If it's cole for me, it must be awf'ly damn cole for them too. And I bleeve I was right."

"Well, they are dogs," she says. "God our Creator gave them fur to keep them warm. They are used to the outside, they are used to the cold."

"Maybe so," Mister Felix says, "maybe so." He ain't done chet neither. "I'm a human beeng and I ain't used to it, I know that. I doan like the cole weather. Never did, for that concern. Dogs, you know, they can't talk and tell you how cole it is."

"Mister Felix," she says, "these dogs are used to it. Gracious, they have hardly ever seen the *inside* of this house in all the years —"

"They like't, look to me," he says back.

But you cain't be short wid her. "Oh, you can't go by that," she says. "They are like these boys here. You give them an inch and they take a country mile. Mama, after Daddy died, she wanted them in the house too."

Mister Felix is set back in the cheer. Back smokin' his seegar. Mizz Henrietta standin' up. Over him, almost. For advantage, I reckon.

"The dogs," she goes on, "were the first sign. I knew right then and there she wasn't right no more in the head. That was the start of all of Mama's troubles. All the other signs, they came later."

I was wond'rin what all the other signs was.

Mister Felix don't say no more. 'Cause he *cain't:* Mizz Henrietta almost got his face in her lap.

Then justthatquick she turnt and went outen the room.

Next day I see for my-self. Doh to his room left open as I pass by. *Two places* where they's hair on the floh. Ain't human beeng hair neither.

The man don't care who knows.

I think Mister Felix was a dog hisself wunst.

Felicissimo

Hadda trust somebody. *Had to,* that's all there was to it.

Those boys, shuck, you could trust them all right, I *bleeve,* but they were only young boys. Kids. Kids doan know so much. Think they do till some-somebody comes along and shows them a diff'rent way to do the things.

I thought Cholly, he gets around the country quite a bit, he's been around the bend a few times I 'magine, he would know best of all what I had in ma head. And keep a secret.

Chewsee, that's how I was think, that was what was go through ma head.

So after supper I took him out to the barn there and I said, "Cholly, I wange you to tell the tru' now. Tell me whatchew think. If it ain't a good idea what I show to you, I wange you speak up. There woont be no hard feelin's."

"Well, show me," he says, "I'm from Missouri."

"Missouri, ma foot," I tole him. Kid.

Ole Man Peele, I din know him, but he was a foxy grandpa as far as I can make out. He had a workbench there and a drawer where I found all kinda junks. All kinds. Man, I never saw so much junk in ma life. He had so damn much junk took me a whole afternoon to go through.

That's where I hid ma secret. I knew zactly where it was.

With Cholly there, I hand him the first teen can I saw. "Okay, Smartypants," I said to him. "Tell me some. How do you open this can?"

He lookt to me, then to the can, then back to me.

"I'd go back in the house," he says, "and find me a can opener. Why? How would *you* do it?"

"I would do same as you," I said. "But just suppose. Suppose we was in war. Fight. What would you do then? You couldn go back in the house. What would you do?"

"I wasn't in the war," he said. "I don't know what they did back then."

"They did't the hard way," I tole him. I din tell him the whole story. "That was no good," I said. "Bad enough haveta fight, don'cha think?"

"That's how I look-ed it," he said to me. I like to hear him talk. He was a country boy. Like me.

"*So would I,*" I tole him. "So I thought to maself, How would you, what would you do to make a teen can open up when the time comes you doan have some to do the job? What would you do, Cholly?"

"Damn if I know, Fee. *Bite* the bastard off if I was hungry enough."

I hadda laugh. "Darn tootin'," I said. "When you get hungry, you wanna eat. Yeah boy. That only stands to reason. But there should be an easy way to go about't. Chewsee ma point?"

"I think so, yeah. So far, I guess so."

"I got an idea in ma head. See whatchew think."

I took a box from the drawer where I had ma *special* can. Inside was another box. Because you can never be too damn sure of anything.

"Watch now," I said, and Cholly was look to me like a little boy.

I took the teen can and I pulled off a little key I had made. Not no housekey. This was no more than a piece of metal, with a hole on the end. That's all was. A re'tangle, attached to the bottom of the can. But it fit into the seam I had made.

What did I do but take the key and attach it to the seam, on the end. I turn. I turn once, twice, three times. Round and round she went. What do you know but the seam came off, in a line, a strip. Now then.

The strip, the seam I'm tellin' you about, came off *so easy.* Nothing to it. What did I do then but push off the top. Use ma thumb.

Peaches inside.

"There's your dessert, Cholly. See if it's any good."

Oh, he *laughed.* He couldn get over.

"Hey! That's some trick!"

"Ain't no trick to it," I said.

He was study, study.

"Now you know ma secret," I tole him. "Doan tell nobody."

"No danger," he says. "But if I's you, I'd get me a patent." I din know what that was, but I had an idea.

"Tell Washington. Make you a fortune next war comes along."

"D.C. Washington," I said. "Lawyers and gyppers. We'll see."

I wasn quite ready to tell ma story. Just that minute I wand to but I still din know maself how I stood to fare with that Cincinnati business. I put that stuff away, but such things as that you never forget.

Like that Red. So sick. Was worry how she made out.

If I tell anybody, I'll tell this Cholly. One of these days.

He was hold the can up to the light. He couldn get over.

"Go on, you rascal you," I tole him, "eat them peaches!"

He did too.

Joe Doakes

Damndest thing I've seen in quite a spell. That Eyetalian gentleman out there wearing Mister Peele's old straw hat, harness around his neck, going to town like nobody's business. Neat row after neat row.

Don't know why Caledonia didn't think of it before this. I know the daughter never would have. Girl hasn't that much imagination *or* business sense. Hasn't a lick of horse sense. I know some men *and* women think she still has her cherry.

So the mother and the daughter got themselves a gardener. Well, they could use one. Handyman to boot, from what I hear. Machinist by trade. Three in one. A bargain by any other name.

Fella came along none too soon. Those vines, they needed cutting bad. Those rosebushes were just growing wild. Can't for the life of me see how people can let things go so. Time was, old Peele, he wouldn't let a week go by when he wasn't out there with his sickle or knife or just himself, bent over, picking.

The daughter, Henrietta, wouldn't part with a nickel to have somebody do it. Not her. Well, she got that from the old man. That and all that money and the means (if she was ever smart enough to see it and ambitious enough to do something about it) to make more of it. The father's gifts to the daughter didn't include intelligence nor ambition.

But stingy? She got that all right.

My God that man was stingy. Even to himself.

He was a man who could own as fine an automobile as there was, but what did he buy and keep but a Model A, still out back in the barn, patched to hell and beyond, all to save a nickel. For most of his life. Then just before he took sick he got that Buick. That don't do nothing but sit, collect dust in the barn, next to the Ford, doing the same thing.

You'd see him walking funny. Feel sorry for him even. Think he had a touch of the rheumatism. I would. Anybody would.

So one day I said to him, I said, "Mister Peele, why don't you see a doctor? Your feet look like they're bothering you a powerful lot."

Why, he looked at me like I was a crazy man. Mouth about flew open. Had bad teeth. Never went near a dentist, it looked like. Just like poor folks.

"Joe," he says, "there ain't a damn thing wrong with my feet. My feet are as good as yourn. What makes you think there is something the matter with my feet?"

I saw he was right agitated about it.

"Sorry, Mister Peele," I said, and I was too. Sorry I had ever brought the matter up. "I guess it was my mistake," I said, doing some quick thinking. "My eyes, they've been bothering me here lately. Maybe I should get 'em checked."

Made him laugh, what I said.

"Save your money," he says. "You don't need to see no damn eye doctor." And he takes off one of his shoes.

"My cardboard, Joe. She shifted on me," he says, "and this got in it." Chucked a stone as big as a shotgun shell. "That's what you saw."

Now he was adjusting his piece of cardboard in his shoes, trying to get it just right, and tying his shoe back up.

"There now," he says, "that'll do me."

Swear on the Bible. A man who could have had his shoes made in England or Italy or even New Yawk or Boston, but he's wearing department store shoes and then he's too tight to get a shoemaker to have them resoled. Family getting, got their money from numerous enterprises — farming in this neck of the woods, dry goods store, renters; tobacco farm down in Southern Maryland — and he'd sooner put cardboard in his shoes than go buy another pair or even get these ones fixed. I swear.

So I can see where the daughter gets it. No, not business sense. *Stinginess.* Betchew that Eyetalian ain't getting so much as a fi'-dollar discount on his rent. Betchew that man ain't getting a damn thing. Not from that woman. He's doing all that work around the place 'cause he wants to do it. No other reason.

Gets a kick out of it, I reckon. Sure wish I had his get-up-and-go. You don't see many with that kind of pep. No indeed.

Have to give credit where credit's due.

Even has that grape arbor up where it was before the storm hit. Back over the barn doors, where it belongs. I've seen him take the hammer and nails out of the barn and do the work. I've seen that man take the plow out and work way past dark, then go to his job bright and early the next morning. I've seen him prune, mend, plow, plant, and now pick.

I see this evening he's got those two boys out yonder to lend him a hand.

Hargrove

We got strawberries this year. The new man's doin'. He plants 'em, he tends 'em, and he picks 'em. Trouble is, he expects me and Levi to pick 'em too.

He over there now, pickin', Mister Felix is.

"Come on, you fellas," he says when he thinks we slack off. And when we say sumpn about it, he says he might haveta tell Mizz Henrietta. When I whisper I might haveta tell who he really is, he comes back and says to me, "You like to eat 'em, don'cha, you Hargrove?"

So here we are after supper. Me and Levi and Mister Felix. Me wantin' to play ball; Levi wantin' to go off somewheres, the woods, any ole place, he ain't pa'tic'lar where, and sing his songs.

We got two colanders. He in one row, me and Levi in another. Mister Felix, he musta been a picker somewhere or else he learnt it in one of his pitcher shows. His hands is fast. Goes about it right bidnesslike.

Sun's pretty well up. Good baseball weather.

I got me a place behind the barn. I got me some chalk and I got me a strike zone. I pitch to the batters there. I call 'em as I see 'em.

Last night I pitched a shutout for eight innings. Then that Babe Ruth comes up in the bottom of the ninth and hits one out. You cain't mess wid him. Cain't make no mistakes. Cain't afford to. But we had us a comf'table lead and won anyway.

Had ma good stuff. All ma pitches was workin'.

So I'm pickin' them berries and thinkin' how I could be pitchin' another mastahful game tonight when I get another idea. I look to the bowl, that colander we have, and I see Levi is too.

That's when we giggle and Mister Felix looks to Levi, then to me. He stands up, pushes his pickin' hat back, ole straw hat he found somewheres on the place, rubs his handkerchief over his face. Has to wear glasses when he picks. Cleans 'em off wid that handkerchief too. No more than a rag when he gets done wid it.

"You boys," he says to me and Levi, "what's so funny? Some's goin' on over there." He knows. You cain't fool that man. Knows all the tricks. Reckon he's done 'em all.

Levi gigglin' behind his hand. Silliness. That boy gives hisself away every time. Face betrays him. You kin jest about read his mind such as it is.

"I hear you over there," Mister Felix says, "hee-hee-hee, hee-hee-hee, like nanny goats." Makes you laugh, that man, way he talks. "Come on, you boys! No time to slack off now!"

Levi leaves it to me to speak up. That boy ain't good but for one thing.

"Boss," I says, plead, "how much we gotta do tonight?"

"Fill your bowl," he says. "That's our agreement."

"We want a new agreement," I tell the man.

"Aw no," Mister Felix says, "none of that stuff. We talk about that tomorow. Bring your lawyer."

"We cain't afford no lawyer," I tell him.

"Doan tell me your trouble," he says. *"Pick!"*

I start to say we be our own lawyers when he says it again: *"Pick!"*

Levi knows what we gonna do. He smart, that way. About the same time as me, he slides over to the bowl Mister Felix has — his back is turnt — and grabs two hands' worf of berries. I'm right behind him. Mister Felix is bent over busy.

When he turns around he right su'prised. Pulls his ole straw hat back and says, "I doan understand't. I pick and I pick. My bowl doan seem to get full. Must be a whole in the bottom."

Looks to me, then Levi. Hisn ain't but half full.

"Maybe it's the rabbits eat 'em," Mister Felix says. "Either I got a hole in ma bucket, or else it's the rabbits. You boys see any rabbits out here?"

"Sometimes," Levi says, "sometimes I see the rabbits out here."

"I reckon they gotta eat too," Mister Felix says.

"*We* doin' jest fine," Levi says, points. "Jest look. Our bowl is gettin' full right quick." Turns his head right quick. "We makin' a good headway."

Mister Felix shakes his head. "Doggone if I know what it is. Must be doggone rabbits. That's all I know. Have to get ma shotgun out and shoot 'em dead."

"You jest haveta pick faster than they kin eat 'em," I says. "If we see any, we be sure and tell you, Mister Felix. The way we work, so fast and clean, we don't have no time for watchin'. Me and Levi, we too busy pickin'."

Good thing Mister Felix's back is turnt 'cause Levi about to fall down laugh so hard. That boy cain't tell a lie and he cain't keep a straight face to save his soul. I don't know what will ever become of him in this world.

We gotta go again. We ain't halfway there chet.

I make motions for Levi to wait 'cause this Eyetalian man, he ain't nobody's fool. We pick a little, not enough to get tard out, 'cause I gotta pitch. I got a new rubber ball to throw against the barn. Bought it wid Groucho's hush money.

I give Levi a nod — that's our signal — and we go again.

He got bofh hands full. I do the same. Our bowl is full if we jigger it.

Mister Felix's back is turnt and he still bent down, pickin'. When he comes up, turns around, and sees his bucket, he says, "Aw-oh. Dawn if they din come back 'round this way again. Hargrove, Levi. Cheewsee?"

Me and Levi, we too busy pickin'. Honest, this time.

"If I ketch 'em," Mister Felix says, "they'll be dead rabbits! We'll have rabbit stew for tomorrow night's supper, I doan mean maybe."

We keep our heads down. Busy. Too busy for talk.

We pick about five more minutes. To make it look good. I make motions for Levi. Our bowl is full. Good job for two young boys. A full pail. Big pail too.

I do the talkin'. Levi, he ain't no talker.

"Boss," I says, "looks like we got a full pail here."

Mister Felix stands up, turns around. Pushes his straw hat back, dries off his glasses. He's sweat. We ain't. We boys.

"I see that," he says. "Funny dawn thing. You boys behind me, and not even far up your row. You got good ones? Doan do no good to pick berries ain't ripe."

"We pick clean," I says, "and four hands is better'n two."

"To be sure," Mister Felix says. "I'll be check, see if all your berries is good."

"Oh, they good, they the best," Levi says, all smiles. It don't pay for that boy to talk.

Mister Felix holds up our bowl. Says, "Yes, *sir!* Looks pretty dawn good to me. Two heads are better'n one any day, to be sure. And I got them rabbits steal from ma bowl. That ain't fair, d'you agree, Levi?"

Levi, he a good one to ask. "No, suh," he says, "that ain't fair."

"Should we take 'em in to Mizz Henrietta?" I ask him.

"By all means," Mister Felix says. "I'll give her ma *re*port tonight. She mi' not know about these rabbits out here."

"Be sure and give her a *good re*port about me and Levi," I tell the man.

"If I doan forget to remember," he says, "yes *sir!*" Jiggles the handkerchief he got around his neck. Man sweats like nobody's bidness.

"Yes, sir," he goes on, "no question about't. You two fellas are some strawberry pickers you are."

Me and Levi, we take our bowl into the house. Mizz Henrietta ain't in the kitchen, but Mizz Caledonia is. She smiling. I dunno why. She do that sometimes.

Outen the patch Mister Felix is bent over pickin', goin' to town wid his pickin'. Man picks like he's workin' for somebody, but I *know* that somebody ain't Mizz Henrietta.

Works fast, moves on till all you kin see of him is that straw hat.

THREE

Crossing the Line

Hargrove

"Peetch that ball," he says. *Peetch.* Way he talks.

I ain't worried about pitchin' that ball. I know I kin pitch that ball. I kin pitch that ball like there's no tomorra. I kin pitch that ball as good as I want, I even tell Mister Felix so.

But it jest so happens this time I miss the strike zone against the barn that I drew wid the chalk I stole that time from the schoolhouse. Him standin' there wid 'em droopy ole lids watchin' me like I'm some kinda pitcher show, no wonder I was high and outside that time.

He laughin'. Says, "Lemme ask you question," and I kin see it comin'. Man don't wait for no answer, he jest goes ahead. Says, "Every time I see you play ball, you play by yourself." Says, "Why is zat?"

He don't know nothin', that man. This ain't Hollywood. This ain't make-believe.

I jest shake my head and go into the stretch. Fastball knicks the corner.

I don't know how, nor why, but I'm the th'owin' the ball faster'n last year. And my curve, th'owed sidewarm like I do, breaks better'n evah. I th'ow one, jest to show my-self how good I am.

I'm good.

Mister Felix still standin' there shakes his head. "Why doan you play in a real game?" he says, no joke.

"This is practice," I tell him, see if that'll satisfy his big ole nose. Maybe he'll leamy alone then. He a nosey somebody.

"I see the boys play," he says, "down the hollow. Pra'tic'ly every night."

"White boys," I tell him. "There ain't enough of us to get up a game. Cain't very well play wid the white boys."

"Oh, is zat so?"

"Yeah," I tell him, low and inside but ovah, "zat's so."

Shakes his head. "You play good," he says. Like he some kinda ex-pert. Don't trust actors. They'll tell you whatevah they think you wanna hear. Just ask ole Henrietta. She'll give you an earful.

"Ain't enough colored boys to get up a game," I tell him. "You see many colored ones 'round these parts, 'ceptin' me and Levi, and he ain't a ballplayer but a singer?"

"Peetch that ball!" he says.

I do. Harder'n befo'. Inside for a strike.

"Pretty dawn good," he says, all su'prised I kin do how I do.

"Tell 'em white folk," I says to him, 'cause he makes you think you kin say what you please, he got that way about him, "and see where it gets you, *Mister Groucho Marx!*"

Puts his fingers to his lips. *"Shhhtt."*

"Fambly," I tell him. "That's some fambly you got. Won't even he'p you out in your hour of need."

"I know't, Hargrove ma boy," he says. "It ain't fair, is it?"

"Durn *unfair,*" I tell him, "but when ain't it?"

Shrugs 'em big ole shoulders. Relights his stogie. Takes a few puffs. Like his brain operate better that way. Smacks his lips together, and that's when he comes out wid it:

"Hargrove," he says, "I bleeve your trouble can be fix."

"Uh-uh," I tell him. "Don't get no idears like that in your head, Mister Felix. Thank you jest the same. I gotta play wid my own people."

"Who's your people, Hargrove?"

Strange question to be askin' me, I thought.

"Colored people," I tell him.

"That ain't fair," he says. "I doan call that sport."

"It ain't," I tell him. "You know it ain't. I reckon even white folk know it ain't. Some of 'em."

"You gotta talk to somebody," he says, "somebody who can change the rules in your favor."

"Change the rules?" I says. He a crazy man, a crazy white man. *"Change the rules?* Did I hear you right? Change the rules," I says. "You from another country, ain't you? You jest get off the boat? How many niggers you got in them pitcher shows you useta be in?"

Shup up then. Man ain't got no answer.

I'm jest th'owin' now, stayin' loose.

"I see whatchew mean," he says after a spell.

"You gonna play wid the men this summer?" I ask him. "They play every summer. You look like you might be fast. I know you strong, but has you got the *eye?*"

"I ain't no ballplayer," he says.

"Don't play ball?" I ask him. "Why is zat?"

"Doan know," he says. "Just doan. Never learned how. That's all."

"You don't *learn* to play ball," I tell him. "You jest do it. Like when you swim. You knows how to swim, don'cha?"

Shakes his head. I don't believe him.

"Doan know how," he says.

I don't believe him. Man's fulla stuff.

"Peetch that ball!" he says.

I th'ow it right down the middle. Hardest ball I th'owed all day, and Gehrig, he swings and misses. I'm th'owin' a lot harder'n last year. I got new stren'th, yes I do!

"You should play on a team," he says.

"I tole you how it is." I seen it befo'. The man, he kin be right slow sometimes.

"Uh-uh," he says. "You heard what I said. Change the rules."

I kin only take so much, but I don't get excited. This Eyetalian man, he ain't right in the head.

"Sure," I says, no useta argue wid him, "you change 'em rules. Change the world too. You're white. Dark white but white."

"All right," he says, fixin' his straw hat that ain't even hisn. "Just a minute and I'll tellya what I'm gonna do."

Walks away. Jest like all the rest. He a talker.

All talk, you ask me.

Big Frankie

I was on the line when the inspectors came today. The new man, the mechanic, he told me they was comin'.

"Hey sis," he says to me. Called me sis. Like we was fambly. "The men in the dress-up suits are here." The inspectors, the guvment inspectors, he meant by that.

So I didn't have no trouble today. It was because the mechanic, he told me.

If he hadn't, *Lordy.* I would have been in hot water, sure. If they catch you, and they have caught some young girls, it does happen, and when it does, brother look out. *Lordy.* If they catch you, everybody catches hell and they won't let us young girls come to work no more.

So I can't get caught. I got to work.

The mechanic saved my neck today. I went to him, same as I do with Mitchell, you know after I came out of the toilet. (The toilet's the best place to hide.) I told the man, "Thank you," but he didn't say nothin' but "Doan mention it."

"You don't want sumpn from me?" I said then.

'Cause Mitchell does. I let the new man know it.

He looked at me a right good while. But then he says, "What is it you think I want, young lady?" Talks funny but you can understand him 'cause he talks so slow. He could be from around here if it wudn't for that.

Then he, I guess he, figgered it out. Shook his head. Smiled. He has a nice smile. Told me his name was Felix. Told him mine was Frankie.

"Frankie?" he says it real slow. "What kinda name is that?"

"I dunno," I told him. "My mama named me Frances." She calls me Franny but I don't like that name so I didn't tell.

"*Ohh,*" he says, like he knew it well. Maybe he did. I couldn't rightly say. "Fran-*chee*-ska." He says it again, just that way, like it means sumpn.

I did not say one word. I liked Fran-*chess*-ka. I thought it was a right nice name.

Everybody else calls me Big Frankie.

But the mechanic, he calls me Fran-*chess*-ka.

I like his way better.

Lulu

I seen him around town. You can't miss him. *Told* Mitchell
I didn't like his looks. I set store by a person's looks and hisn I
didn't trust from the first time I laid eyes on him.

"Foreigners," I told Mitchell. "You cannot trust foreigners.
Half the time you don't know if they know what you mean. The
other half the time you don't know what they mean."

I told Mitchell. "You cannot trust a foreigner." (Half the time
you can't trust Mitchell neither.)

I told him, I said, "Make him pay, first."

"Nah," he says. *Nah.* "That ain't necessary, not with this
fella. I work with this one. What he does, I know he's got the
jack."

With all fellas, it's necessary. I don't care who they are.
That's been my experience. You gotta get the business end outa
the way, first.

Mitchell, I figger him for a smart fella. He tells me he knows
him good and he'll do right by me.

"Nice fella," he says. "No rough stuff."

"All right," I said. Stupid me. I shoulda asked, How good do you know him? How long? But Michell, well, I can't altogether blame Mitchell. He ain't as smart as he likes to make out.

All I can figger is he forgot to tell the wop how it works. Prob'ly told him it was a sure thing but not the catch and there's always a catch. Mitchell's always so busy cookin' up deals sometimes he forgets the details. You never know what he's up to from one minute to the next. It's always sumpn with him because he's a schemer and for that reason at least half the time you can't really trust him.

But money's money and I need the money.

Some people born and raised here don't have the two nickels to rub together and this devil calls for me in a shiny, looked-to-be brand-new car. Dress suit. Put you in the mind of Valentino, that's how good-lookin' he was. Kinda looks you don't trust, if you know what's good for you. Nice, polite as can be. I figger he knows a thing or two. Mitchell says he has the jack. I don't know. Sounds too good to be true.

I need the money. It's always the money.

Took me to the pitcher show. The show was all right. Edward G. Robinson. My Valentino calls him a sawed-off shotgun. Made me laugh at the time.

Afterwards, we all went out to eat. We had that Elmer and another girl works for Mitchell with us. Thelma. Mitchell works with Elmer and Valentino, but I don't think he knows Valentino all that good, even if he does work with the man.

My date has it all over Thelma's in the looks department. But Thelma told me later Elmer did all right by her when they finished up in the room. Which is more than I can say.

That damn Eyetalian. Big nose. Big wowow. He satisfies himself once, twice, three times. Takes longer and longer each time. I try to hurry him up, but it don't do no good. "What's your rush, ma'am?" he says.

Then he made me good and mad. Says to me, "Whatsamatter? You eat too much supper?" I coulda killed him there on the spot.

Funny thing was, I didn't think he was ever gonna start. Come to find out, once you got him a-goin', you couldn't hardly stop him. But I did. I put my foot down.

There he was, lovin' me up, fixin' to go again. I didn't know how long he was good for, and I was in no mood to find out. I was wore out.

"Save it, big boy," I told him. "Tomorrow night's another night. We're all done for tonight. I gotta find out what the deal is here."

"What deal is zat, ma'am?" he says. Dumb as all get-out. Says it as dumb as any country boy on this side. Just that dumb. Says it again: "What deal is zat, ma'am?"

"*The jack,*" I tell him, tryin' to keep patience. "Nobody gets sumpn for nothin' in this country. You better learn that right now."

Honestlee, you shoulda seen the look come over that man's face. He didn't seem to understand or maybe he just did. He was kinda cute, I give him that. But that don't pay the rent.

I stepped into my panties. Big smile all over his face again, watchin' me like a hawk. I wanda slap him. He was cute, and I'll say this for him: He was the clearnest man I was ever with, and that includes Preacher, my first, if you can call that one a man.

But a deal's a deal. Even if this Eyetalian don't understand it any more than I do right this minute.

I told him straight up: "I want my money."

"What money is zat?" he says.

I said to him, "You been enjoyin' yourself, ain't you?"

"Very much so," he says.

"Well, honey," I said, "us girls gotta eat too."

"I doan know whatchew talk," he says. "You done et your supper, ain't you?"

"You don't get a sumpn for nothin' in this country, Mister." That was the second time I hadda tell him.

He thinks it's all a joke. "Is zat so?" he says. "You doan mean it."

"Damn right," I told him. I wasn't gonna let him make a damn fool outa me.

"I bought you supper," he says. "I took you to the show. And that lets it out."

And that lets it out. I couldn't see straight. All I saw was red.

"You gotta pay for your pleasure," I told him.

"Is zat so?" he says. "You mean to tell me you din get no pleasure?"

He was still smilin'. All this time. Damn, he could make me mad. His smilin' like that made me mad as hell. Where'd he get off? I didn't know if he didn't know, or what. That broken English didn't help none.

"You don't get it for free," I told him. "That wasn't our bargain."

"I din make no bargains," he says.

Not mean nor nothin'. Just that simple.

"We'll see about that, Mister," I said.

"Here, now," he says. "You should fineesh whatchew you start."

"We're all done here," I told him. "Good and done for."

"Aw, have a heart," he says.

"I'm getting dressed, sport."

Oh, I was mad. He liked me. I can always tell. He liked me a lot, from the look of him. But I couldn't figger this one out. And he was damn nice too. But that don't keep a girl in coffee and cakes.

"Din we go to supper?" he says. "Din we go to the picture show tonight?"

He thought that was my pay. He thought that was all there was to it.

"Listen you," I said, "you pay me or I'll go to Mitchell. He'll get it outaya."

Looked at me a good long while. Them long lids. Cover most of his eyes. Looked a little sleepy-eyed even before we had our shots. That was his natural look, I reckon. But them lids, they can go so far back in his head, and his eyes is so deep-set. He could be the devil himself, lookin' thataway.

"Gawhead," he says. He saw through me. "Tell Meester Mitchell. Ain't nobody stop you."

"This ain't how it's posta work," I told him. "You already dipped your wick I don't know how many times I can't keep account and now you say nothin' doin', no pay? Wuddia take me for, a sap?"

He says it again: "You should fineesh whatchew start." Course he has that funny accent too. But he was just as calm, polite as could be. He wanted some more. Sure, I wanted to, but business is business. A deal's a deal. It was all spoilt for me now anyway.

I buttoned up my dress and fixed my hayer and put on my hat. In the meer I looked like a Sunday school teacher, a rayglar church lady. Like my mama was.

He looked funny, comical. Standing there all bewildered with no clothes on. No, he didn't know what was what. Maybe he was just dumb. Dumb like a fox maybe. Damned if I know. I know I was damn good and mad. I liked him too. Kinda cute, even if he was the devil. But a deal's a deal.

"I'm tellin' Mitchell. Oh, you'll be hearin' from Mitchell."

He didn't say shit. He wouldn't. Just stood there watchin' me and smilin' and hard as arn. I didn't know what was gonna happen next.

"He'll get my money," I said, "because lemme tellya sumpn, Mister. If I don't get my money he don't get his money neither and we all gotta make a livin'. Even us girls."

"To be sure," he says. I can't tell if he's jokin' me or serious. Burns me up! God damn these foreigners!

I told him, I said, "Unless you and that half pint cooked up a deal between yourselfs. Which oughtna su'prise me in the least. Youse two coulda cooked up a deal and conveniently forgot to tell Lulu. Oh, God damn that Mitchell. God damn you too, you big-nosed wop. God damn all men."

I think that convinced him to put his clothes back on.

"Is zat so?" he says. *"C'mon now.* Cheer up."

Easy for him to say.

"Meester Mitchell," he says, "he runs the ball team in town?"

"How should I know? He's got his fingers in a lotta pies. Don't *you* know? You and him are in cahoots, ain't you?"

"I doan know whatchew talk," he says. "You tell your Meester Mitchell when you do your talk Felix wants to see him. Cange you do that?"

"Tell him yourself," I said. "Youse two work together, don'cha?"

"Listen, sis," he says, and he ain't smilin' this time, "you wange your money you think I owe you, cor-rect? Well, then. You do like I tell you."

"It's a damn dirty trick," I said.

"Maybe so. You do like I tell you," he says, like he's my lord and master. "You'll talk to Mitchell before I do. And doan worry. You'll get all's come to you if you got some come to you."

"What lousy luck," I told him. "A skinflint in a brand-new suit and a fancy car. Don't that beat all. I reckon you won't take me home now neither. I reckon I gotta walk."

"Oh no," he says. Says it so low I can barely make it out. "Oh no, sis," he says louder and he smiles. "It's too far to walk. Suppose some strange man comes along and tries to pick you up? Then what?"

I'm doing a slow burn. Funny man. He's a scream.

"I'll buy you some to eat, if you're hungry," he says.

"I done et," I told him, "thank you very much." He had some nerve. Thought he was funny.

"Gimme a minute and I'll tellya what I'm gonna do," he says. Oh, he's happy as a clam. Nothin's botherin' that man.

"You're a big-hearted Joe, ain't you?"

"Oh, how you talk," he says, havin' a swell time.

That smartypants. He's a good one to talk. I nearly laughed in his face. I did, later. *Right in his face.* And wouldn't you know? He got mad. Wasn't mad all this time and he got mad over nothin'.

Had started to put his clothes on. In his good sweet time — he's only got one speed — and I hadda laugh.

He had his draws put on inside out and the pee hole out back.

Harder I laughed, madder he got.

Got so mad he wouldn't talk no more till he let me out. "Doan forget now," he says. "You tell Mitchell what I tole you. Since you insist."

I told Mitchell soon as I got in the door. "No matter what I said, he wouldn't go for it."

I didn't know what to make of Mitchell. He's all for bein' friends. Says, "I'll take care of you." Calls it a mix-up and tells me to help myself to his Jack Daniel's on the dresser.

That ain't the Mitchell I know.

"Let's let bygones be bygones," he says, and rolls over.

You can't trust that man even halfway.

Felicissimo

I doan like to owe nobody. I pay ma debts, then go here, there, anywhere I please without a care in the world. I doan owe nobody, not a damn cent, and anybody says some diff'rent can kiss ma royal.

So I was hate like hell to tell that girl no dice when she was so damn sure, *posateeve,* I owe her some. She was so damn sure, that hot pot, I stop and thought to maself: Uh-uh, brother. Some fishy here somewhere.

And damn if there ain't.

Din wait for Mitchell: *I* went to see *him.* Monday morning, bright and early.

Din have to look far, or very long, for that concern. He was a big smokono. Had to have that damn weed in his mouth or bust. So I never had no trouble to find him.

Mitchell, he took one look at me and he knew why I was come to see him. Din do a damn thing, that Bolshaveek, but stand up and walk the other way.

Oh, he was another smart guy. I could ketch him, but shuck, I din even try.

I thought to maself, You duck me once, brother, but I'll be damn if you'll do twice.

So sure enough ten o'clock come around when they take they break. He was set't the table there, by hisself, just wait. Smoke. He knew I wanda see him, and he was all prepare for. *He thought.*

"What say, Fee?" Oh, he's feel pretty good. Make out like there ain't a damn thing wrong between us.

"Meester Mitchell," I tole him, "I wanna see you."

"See me, here I am," he says. Oh, he's a smart guy all right. Woont look me in the eye. 'Cause he knew I had a bone to pick. He wasn fool me for one minutes. If he thought so, he was mistake.

"That girl," I said, "Lulu." And he starda shake his head, smile. "Turned out to be some lulu all right. She thinks I owe her money. Got mad as hell at me, night before last. Did she tell you?" I knew damn well she did.

"All a misunderstanding," he says. "That's all it was, Fee."

I tole him: "I'll be frank with you, Mitchell: I din like one damn bit what happ between us."

"You know women, Fee. She was pretty hot," he says, laughs, "but she'll get over it. They all do. I told her to let bygones be bygones."

"I doan blame her for be hot," I said, "if you tell her one thing, then turn around and tell me some else. I doan blame her one damn bit. I doan call that fair."

"Nothing to lose sleep over," he says.

"I can go to sleep anytime," I tole him. He knew what I mend.

Threw up his hands. "Just a whore, Fee."

"No matter," I said, "she works for a livin', same as anybody else. Made me mad when I had time to stop and think. That girl, she can't better herself. Doan know no other way, I suppose, than on her back. But you, you damn fool, you know better. Was no talk about money when you spoke to me. Am I right or wrong?"

"I told her what youse did was y'all's business. That's all I said. I swear."

"Your swear doan mean beans to me, Mitchell."

He was smoke like nobody's business.

"That girl," I said, "I suppose she took't the wrong way?"

"I reckon she did," he says. "You'd have to ask her. Cheap whore's trick, you ask me."

Says: "Fee, I told you what she was."

"You never said a damn —"

"Not in so many words maybe. I thought you could put two and two together."

"Your two and two," I said, "makes five."

"Now, Fee, I said I could get you a girl anytime you wanted. As long as the big cheese didn't get wind of it. The big cheese. You know who I mean, don'cha? The old Jew."

"I ain't got no trouble with that man," I said. "All ma trouble is with you."

"I know he likes you," he says. "Took a shine to you right from the start. Be worth it to him, I reckon, if you got a girl every night. Somebody to keep you from gettin' idears about that secretary of hisn. That Rosalie. 'Cause she can't keep her eyes off you. Everybody's seen it. Old Jew, I reckon he has too. You oughta give her a try, Fee. I'd like some of that, myself."

That struck him funny, I doan know why.

"I doan know whatchew talk," I said. You couldn bleeve a damn thing was come outa that mouth.

But he kept't up. Says, "If that old Jew found out I was makin' money on the side, on comp'ny time, I'd be out on my ear. He'd fire me just as quick as he did poor Pooch. You know he would."

"That only stands to reason," I said.

Smile went away. Bleeve he starda worry then.

"So are you gonna blab? You ain't out nothin' for that girl."

I had no intaynshun to tell the big boss. The idea never even cross ma mind. But I din let on.

"You louse," I tole him. "I din know I was suppose to pay. That wasn part of our agreement. But I'll tell you what I'll do with you, Mitchell. 'Cause we're such good friends, two peas in a pod. I woont say nothin' and you keep your job. Both jobs."

Smile came back. He was feel pretty good again.

"On one condition."

Smile was gone bye-bye. Smoke was come outa his mouth like't was on fire. But that doan stop him from talk. "I ain't so sure I like the sound of this," he says.

I tole him, "I doan care if you like or doan like."

He shut up for a minutes or two.

"Mitchell," I said, "tell me some. You're a big shot in this town. Anyway, that's what a little bird tole me. Have a ball team. Young boys play. Am I right or wrong so far?"

"Oh yeah," he says, "that part's right. Play ball all over the county. Took the title last year."

"I doan give a damn what the hell you did last year," I said. "That's no concern a-mine. Ma point is this: You're the manajeer. The big shot. You agree with me on that part?"

He nodded. I knew he would. Then he starda think.

"Little bird you met up with has a big mouth," he says, disgustopated. "Name of Lulu, no doubt."

"Nevermind that," I said. "In the house where I stay —"

"The Peele place. I know it. Everybody does."

"Liss to me," I tole him. "There's a boy there. A color boy. Can throw that damn ball —"

He wouldn even let me fineesh what I starda say. Was shake his head before I could spit it out.

Well that made me mad.

"Liss to me, you . . . *pimp*," I tole him. "You doan shake your head when I'm talk. *First of all.*"

Stop shake his head justthatquick. He knew I was ready to knock his block off. Kept smoke, though. He sure like to smoke, that Bolshaveek.

"Here's what I'll do with you," I said. "You put that boy on the ball team and you can be King Shit for all I care."

"I don't get it," he says. I can see that. "Wuddia care about some nigger kid out at the Peele place?" He can't shut up. "Who's puttin' you up to this? Commonists? They're troublemakers, Fee. The damn Commonists'll put this country on the bum yet. They got you over a barrel, Fee? They makin' you say these damn fool things? 'Cause if they are, I know some people —"

"I doan know no Communeests," I said, "but I know a Bolshaveek when I see one."

Act like he din hear. "Fee, wuddia suppose people's gonna think if I do what you want? Answer me that."

"Doan tell me your trouble," I said.

"Wuddia think they'll do to me?"

"I doan know," I tole him, "and I doan care."

I could see he was think about some. Some scheme, I imagine.

Sure enough, he was. "You won't haveta pay for a girl as long as you live around here," he says. "I'll fix it with Lulu. Bet she didn't show you what-all she can do with that mouth. Saves that for her longtime clients. Drives 'em crazy, dying for more. Think about it, Fee."

"I never hadda pay for a girl in ma life, Meester, thank you just the same. *Before I forget.*" Got out ma wallet, hand him a twenty-dollar beel. "First time for everything, I reckon. Be sure that girl, she gets what's come to her, Mitchell."

Grab that money like a bird near starve in the wintertime. Remind me of the pigeons I wanda feed my last day in Cincinnati. Better comp'ny, to be sure.

"You wouldn't have to pay, Fee. Think it over. It's the best I can do." About plead.

"Try harder," I tole him.

Says, "Fee, you don't know what you're askin'."

"I ain't askin'," I said, "I'm tellin'. You do like I'm tell you, and your trouble is over. If you doan, then brother, your trouble is just stard. I'll go to the big boss and tell him the whole story. Your second job, on comp'ny time. How you do these young girls. You should be ashamed. So's up to you, ma friend. You do, or else."

Stop smoke. Shake his head how a machine does. Says: "You damn dago red."

I knew that was come. Like I ain't heard that before.

"Oh, how you talk," I said. That got his goats up.

"You'll turn the game into a damn circus freak show," he says, plead now. "The players, the parents, the people in town, hell, the whole damn county'll take matters into their own hands!"

"You see to it that they doan, Mitchell. Now I'm cound on you. Doan let me down."

"He better be damn good."

"Wait till you see. He can throw that ball," I said. "No question about't."

"I hope he's all you say. Damn you, Fee. I can't do it on my own. I'll have to talk to some people. Maybe they'll go for it, if he can toss that apple."

"See that you do," I said. "You're a good talker."

"Maybe they'll let him in." Seemt like he was talk to hisself. "For an inning or two. In a game that's already lost." Finely he hadda let it out. Says, "Jesus H. Christ! Not an outfielder, not even a pinch hitter. You want him on the mound."

Was shake his head a mile a minute but wasn act so smart now.

"Now then," I said. "Now we understand each 'n' other?"

Nod. "But wuddia care, Fee?" Plead some more. Made you sick to see. "Why you wanna upset the applecart? Tell me that, fella."

"You tend your own business," I said, "and I'll tend yours."

"Ah, more double talk," he says, disgustopated. "I can't figure you out."

"All the boys can play," I said, "and he can't? You call that fair? You call that sport? I doan."

Shakes his head some more, looks the other way, disgustopated. I doan care, for maself, how he takes it.

"I'll be keep ma eye on you from now on," I said.

He said some, I doan know what, under his breath. I couldn make out what't was and I din care. He wasn man enough to say to ma face, so to hell with him.

"Pay that girl her money," I tole him, "and doan get too big for your breeches, Meester Mitchell."

Made out like he din hear me. Like ma brother Mike used to do. I knew better: He was hear me all right.

The other people, they starda come in, take they break.

I left him set't the table, smoke.

He knew some people, Mitchell tole me. Tole me twice.

Walk away I was wonder: *What kinda people does he know?*

Big Frankie

I gotta do like Mitchell says, Mitchell says.

I don't want to but I'll be in big trouble if I don't. But I'll be in big trouble if I do like Mitchell says.

Stay out of trouble. That's what Frankie has to do.

I don't have a choice, Mitchell says. No two ways about it, the man says. No buts to it, he says.

That Eyetalian man never did me no harm. Told me when the inspectors come around. Saw me with cans of beans in my pockeybook and never let on. That time he took me home in his cah when it was so cold out. Right often took me home when we had that spell of rainshowers. (The girls all lookin' at me. And jealous? *Lordy!*)

Never wunst asked me to do him. Never asked me no favors. Kept his hands off me.

Mitchell says there's things I dunno. Things people don't know about Mister Felix. Says he's a troublemaker.

"What kinda trouble does he make?" I asked him.

"Upsets the applecart," Mitchell says. "You just do what I tell you. You still want to make your money on the side, don'cha? Then do like I tell you, girl."

"Don't I always do like I'm told?" I says back.

"Usely," he says. "Usely you do. But this feller has you under some kinda spell. You and a lot of others around here. He's got you all buffaloed."

I begged that man. "Aw, Mitchell, please," I said. "Can't you get somebody else?"

"You do it," he says, "and see it's done right."

I was cryin'. "But he never made me —"

"You do like I tell you, "Mitchell says. "Or the next time the guvment men come by I'll tell them about a certain fifteen-year-old gal oughta be in school."

I got my mother and my little sisters to think about, he says.

My mother works takin' in laundry and my father takes and sleeps and takes some more.

Mister Felix is the first man I knowed didn't just take all the time. Wouldn't take what was his for the askin'.

"You and me gotta sweet little thing goin', Missy," Mitchell says. "So why be a Dumb Dora? You want to get them teeth all fixed, don'cha? Be like the movie stars?"

I'm only fifteen and my teeth is rotten, front and back. Mitchell won't let me forget. Reminds me every chance he gets. Big joke, to him.

I don't need no reminders. I know I ain't a movie star.

"All you gotta do," Mitchell says, "is let him take you home in his car. Make sure people see you. Wave to 'em. Say 'G'night girls' like you do."

"What else?" I ask. 'Cause I know it ain't all I gotta do. 'Cause I know Mitchell.

Mitchell's starin' at me right hard. "You go to the police," he says. "Townies. Ask for Sergeant Daggett. D-a-g-g-e-t-t. He's the only one you wanna talk to. Daggett."

"And then? What do I do then?"

"You're gonna tell Daggett how a man from work forced hisself on you. You don't know his name."

"Everybody knows his name."

"All right, say his name. But make sure you tell Daggett how he looks, the way he talks."

Calls me Fran-*chess*-ka. Tell him that too?

"What about Mister Felix?" I ask.

"Forget Mister Felix," Mitchell says. "You'll be workin' two jobs and feedin' mama and the little ones. Even get them rotten teeth of yourn fixed up. Someday, I reckon."

"Suppose it don't rain this week," I say, hopin'.

"Oh, it'll rain," Mitchell says, so sure of hisself and smilin' big. "If not this week, then the next. What's wrong with you, girl? It's summetime!"

I see his teeth they rotten too.

Lulu

Had me a date last night with a college man. Glorified office boy, come to find out. Calls himself Junior Williams. Just a tall, skinny drink of water, but the kinda somebody who liked himself a lot.

I liked his car. Nice machine, the kind you can take the roof off it. Everything's fine as frog's hair till we come to a field. Boys out yonder playin' ball.

College man, this Junior, he stops the car so quick I thought my head was a-goin' through the winda. Jumps outa the car to make sure he don't need even stronger glasses than the pair he's already got on his head.

So sure enough, I coulda told him, there ain't nothin' wrong with my eyes, there's a niggerboy out there in the field. Just one. He's the pitcher.

This big shot, he's fit to be tied. Starts cursin' up a storm. Curses like there ain't no tomorra. Kicks the weeds with his brand-new, shined-up shoes.

Didn't like what he saw, I reckon.

Comes back to the car cursin'. Opens the glove compartment and takes out a pint and rips the seal open with his nice white teeth.

Me, I don't even folly baseball.

Takes a swig. "Hold this," he tells me. My lord and master.

Starts the car up and drives over the weeds to the ball field. Stops the car, gets out. Trusting soul. Leaves me to hold the pint. Mitchell musta told him I can take it or leave it.

Surprise, surprise. Who is there but Mitchell in the flesh. (Maybe my eyes aren't as good as I think they are. Or maybe Mitchell was behind a tree. I wouldn't put it past him.)

College boy and Mitchell know one another it looks real good. College is givin' Mitchell an earful. Says *shit*. Every other word outa his mouth is *shit*. Outa those nice white teeth.

When he can get a word in edgewise, Mitchell's got his mouth a-goin' a mile a minute, all hush-hush. Whatever it is, they both agree on it. It ain't baseball.

Mitchell, he seen me when he come up, walks back to the car with Junior. Hands me an envelope, turns around, walks back to the baseball. Like I ain't good enough to talk to in broad daylight.

Two fi'-dollar bills inside. For that Felix, I figger. So here I am again, not knowin' the deal.

Junior comes back to the car all smiles. Whistlin'. Turns out he's some talker. Tell you his whole life story as soon as jump in the bed. If all he had to do for a livin' was talk, he'd never go without a meal.

Comes over here from Oakland. Nice little pony ride. Says he's got a girl over there. At first he won't say who, and I don't ask too many questions 'cause it ain't good business. So I didn't say no more.

Didn't need much coaxin', that boy, 'cept to hurry him to get in the bed. Which come to find out is the back seat of his automobile.

Well, no two nights is alike.

Tells me about his girl. Baby, her name is. I thought he was goin' on about a child, when he first come out with it. Baby this, Baby that. But no, Baby's a big girl. She's her daddy's big little girl.

"And who's her daddy?" I ask, natural enough.

Couldn't say. I let it go at that. That pint, I thought, that pint'll get it outaya.

Which it did, when he had killed it about half the way, and out of nowhere he lets go with some more of his curse words and that *shit* again. I hate that word. I only say it when I'm good and mad.

Says, "That damn Bart Lawrence! He won't give me a chance!" And he's about to bawl.

I was wonderin' how many farmers and shopkeepers on Main Street said the same thing, or thought it, over the years, in just that tone. 'Cause it was Bart Lawrence the banker he meant. Everybody lives here knows the name.

So he gives himself away, like I knew he would. Miss Baby Lawrence, he meant. Drivin' 'round town in her fine little car, in her nice dress clothes, livin' under her daddy's roof still.

He was with me to get what she wouldn't, or wasn't allowed to, give him.

But watchin' Junior take another slug from the bottle, which he won't even offer a lady, I thought to myself, There's more to it than that. 'Cause I ain't seen her in a good long while.

I figgered it out then, about the envelope. It was from *him*. Fancied himself too good to hand it to me. Not knowin' is one thing; bein' ignorant's another.

Sonny, I thought, you're Bart Lawrence all over again, only you don't know it, and it's too damn bad you can't get any, and you won't till you put that pint down.

Which he did there in the car when he was done with it. I heard it go *swish* through the weeds and *plunk* when it hit the ground. I was lookin' at the stars.

But that ain't that the end of his troubles. If I was to bet I'd put money down that Baby ain't no more virgin than yours truly, and this Junior's got bigger problems than a pint and quick piece can fix.

If I'm wrong I hope Baby don't expect much.

But it don't take much to get a gal in a fambly way.

College man, I was thinkin' while the stars was blinkin', you're just dumb enough to get somebody in a whole lotta trouble.

Big Frankie

Rain, rain, go away. Come back another day.

I finish my cigarette. With the women. Big help, they are. They hate me anyways. I can feel they hate. They oughta know how hard it is. They of all people. Say they do but they don't.

"You won't ever see me stoopin' to what you do, Frankie."

"Take a stick to that old man of yourn while he's in the bed. Or else when he first gets up. Su'prise him. Give him the su'prise of his life. *I* would."

That's what they say. All pretty brazen, talkin' big on they break. Over they cigarettes. When the whistle blows, they all go back to work. Same as me. We are the same then.

Steady rain outside since I come to work. Warm summer rain. Like pee. A girl could walk home in it with an umbrella. Wisht I had me an umbrella.

Maybe somebody 'sides Mister Felix will come along. Another nice man.

Poor man. Wonder what kinda trouble he got into with Mitchell.

I cain't be responsible. Like the men say to us girls. Man got his own self in trouble. Not on my account. On his own. By his own doin's.

Mitchell says we all gotta look out for ourselves. Says that's what he does.

No foolin'.

I gotta look out for myself and my mama and my baby sisters. The little ones. The all-right ones. I don't care about Poppy. Hit him and I'd go to jail. *The law.* The law wouldn't do me no good. He'd just be back again.

This is my life.

Make the best of it, Mama says. Like she done.

So along comes a stranger like nobody else. And I gotta do him dirty. I do'wanna but I gotta look out for me. He don't look out for me other than to give me a ride home. When it rains.

My teeth hurts so.

Jew man comin' 'round. Says we gotta work late.

I'm so glad to see the Jew I don't know what to do.

Gettin' light out too. The sun, I hope.

Caledonia

This was upstairs here, before church on Sunday.

"That boy Levi," I said, "hasn't he a wonderful singing voice?"

"A gift from God," she said, watching herself in the mirror. "But such a queer boy. I hear him sometimes, out there in the woods, making up his songs."

"Loud enough to bust your eardrums."

"He'd be welcome in any church choir," I said. "Pity the boy has no church of his own to go to."

She looked at me for the longest time before she came away from the mirror.

"Mama," she said, "where ever did you get such an idea?"

"That boy is some Caruso, sure enough."

"Landsakes, Mama, he can sing. That's a fact. And I agree with you. He oughta be in his own church. He'd be most welcome —"

"Around here," I said, "there is no such church."

"Levi, in our church?" she said, her face in front of mine, moving but not smiling. "Honestly, Mama, where did you ever get such an idea?

"Too doggone bad nobody else can hear that Levi."

"Mister Felix," I said, making my mistake. "He thought of it. We got to talking after supper one night."

The words of the devil came out out of her mouth then. Calling me a disruption to her life. A burden placed on her shoulders for God-only-knows what reason.

I realize now, too late: If I had left that man's name out of it, Henrietta would not be carrying on so. Poor fellow. I reckon I got Mister Felix in Dutch by the very mention of his name.

"He does almost as good as I can, doan you think?" He loves *to play the fool, that man.*

"That man," Henrietta was saying, "has his hands — and other things — in too many pies."

I don't know what she means.

"It's scandalous," Henrietta said, "what the man is doing. They got Hargrove playing on the white boys' baseball team. Nobody can prove it, but the talk in town is he's behind it in some way."

Ranting and raving, panting, my daughter.

"A total stranger. A body who didn't even grow up here having so much say that he can get a colored boy on the whites' team. I know he's behind it. I just know it."

She knows so much, my daughter.

"You have your style," I said, kidding back.

"He's done wonders around here," I said. "The man has a green thumb, just like your daddy!"

"You don't mention that man in the same breath!"

"I wasn't speaking disrespectfully, I was only —"

"Oh Mama, you are such a burden, such a burden."

"But look around you," I said, saying too much, talking more than I have in ever so long, "look at all the work he's done. A professional gardener, a professional couldn't do better —"

"Thank you, ma'am. I'm glad you like't."

"Oh Mama, you don't know. They way he's going about it, that man'll have this place looking like some Eyetalian villa. It won't even look like our home no more."

"The rosebushes, the grape arbor, the vegetable garden!"

"He's taking over! His kind, that's what they do. They come over here and they take over!"

I spoke calmly, to calm her. "He's made the place come alive again."

Shook her head. "You don't know the half of it, Mama." It worked: She was calm. "How that man tramps in all kinds of dirt from outside. Takes his bath and leaves a ring 'round the tub for me with my aching back to clean up after. Mercy me! There are none so blind as those who will not see."

And he has such a nice smile.

"Talk to Pastor Hall, about Levi," I said. "See what he says. He's a man of God."

"Getting late, I have to go now, Mama. I am a wreck," she said. "I don't need a mirror to tell me. You and that strange man have made a wreck of me this morning. I don't know what else a decent Christian body can do to overcome the devil. *And I thought you were getting better, Mama.*"

Poor Henrietta. A pity to be so distraught on such a bright and sunny Sunday.

I can see, from up here, some of her friends and the neighbors join her. All dressed to the nines. On their way to church on a cheerful Sunday morning.

∎

From here, I can even see the church steeple. It's a lovely view, although a bit tiresome after three days.

Her silence hurts me more than these ropes she has placed on me.

I miss Levi singing.

I miss my smiling friend.

Felicissimo

Set't the table, I knew some was fishy. Some din feel just right to me. You know, set't the table and doan nobody talk? I doan call that right.

The ole lady, she din come down to supper. Two, three days pass by and I ain't seen her. When I ask where she was, somebody, I forget who, said she was sick. *Sick ma eye.* I knew some was up. I wasn quite sure, but I was feegure to find out pretty damn quick, 'cause nobody can keep the secrets, 'specially that woman, the Queen Bee, I call her.

So after supper I was set in the room there. Smoke. Digest ma food. Mind ma own business. Just me, by maself.

Who should come in but the big little daughter. Henrietta. Oh, she was mad. I never saw a grown woman so mad as that in ma life. She din like seegar smoke, but that din stop her this time. Plain to see some was up.

"Set down," I tole her, "you rock the boat."

She din think that was funny. But she set down just the same.

"Mister Felix," she says, "I want to talk to you."

"Go right ahead," I said, "I'ma liss."

"My poor mother," she says. "She and I, Mama and I, we had a terrible fight. Just hellacious."

So there't was. But there was more, to be sure.

"Sorry to hear," I tole her. Was too. 'Cause I doan like to see fight.

"She's very angry at me, Mister Felix."

Shut up then but only for a minute, less.

"And you, sir, are the cause of it."

Well that made me mad, but I din say so. Din get a chance.

"In fact," she was say, "you are the cause of most of my troubles. Ever since you set foot in this house. It's been one thing after another."

I blew smoke from ma seegar. Away from her, course. She doan like seegar smoke.

"I doan know whatchew talk," I said. "I doan look for trouble. Mind ma own affairs. Work here, work there. Pay ma room and board on time. Clean up after maself. I doan see what's the trouble, young lady."

I din neither.

She shut up then. But not for long.

"No," she says. "Yes," she says.

Crazy woman couldn make up her mind. Then she spit it out.

"You are one of the best boarders we ever had here."

Lookt like it was hurt her to say. Had trouble to set in the chair. Move her backside one way, then the other. Like a dog has fleas.

"And I know you are a good man, for the most part."

I din know what she mend by that and I din ask.

"But you have funny ways," she says.

I wanda laugh but I din. That was the pot call the kettle black.

"Ways people around here don't understand. Why, Pastor Hall and I even spoke of it."

"I never met him," I said.

She got all excited. "Maybe you should!" she says, I doan know why. "Maybe you should!"

I din say a word. I let her do the talk.

"What we decided — the reverend and I — is that you, your people? You don't know all our ways. Our customs and traditions. You don't mean to do bad things, but I'm afred children and old ladies don't understand much better than you do how things are, how things stand."

"I doan know whatchew talk," I said. I din neither. That's the Christ's truth.

She was about to bust. "You gotta stop putting ideas in people's heads, Mister Felix. That's all there is to it. Landsakes. You and my mother too. Poor Mama. She's just as im*pray*shionable as these colored boys. And she was never like that till you got here.

"You mean well," she was go on, "but neither of you know how times are. Times are *hard*. My mother, weak in the head like she is. These boys, they don't know from nothin', Mister Felix. *I do hate cigar smoke."*

I din say what was go through ma head. I just set there, think a minute, smoke.

Next time she spoke up was so slow, so easy. Made you think she was talk to a baby. (I ain't no baby.) Talk so sweet. Made you sick.

"It's hard for you, new to the country, I understand," she was say. "I truly do. No family. Nobody like yourself. That talks the same language, I mean. It must be very, very lonely. The reverend made me see. He explained to me about your people. About where you come from, how you are."

Talk right, I thought to maself, cange you?

"And how am I?" I said to her. "I'm same as you. The people where I come from *are* who they are. Me, I'm me. Same as you're you. Your mother's your mother."

She was shake her head back and forth. Remind me of machine.

"See how you are? *Do you see?"*

I bleeve she was a little nootsy, that woman.

After a minutes or two, I said, "No, I doan. How am I?"

"Mister Felix," and she was laugh like a crazy woman, "you do try my patience like nobody else."

"Doan get disgustopated on ma account," I tole her.

"Oh, no," she says, stop laugh, "that would be wrong. Before I thought you were awnree. But you're not an awnree man, Mister

Felix. I know that now after talking with the reverend —you really should meet Pastor Hall — and our little talk tonight."

"How can you be sure?" I said.

"Now, Mister Felix. How you love to kid. *Shhh.*" Talk to me again like I was a baby. "Let me talk," she says. "You promise?"

I din see no way to stop her.

"All right," I said, "I'ma liss."

"A small favor," she says, "that's all I ask."

Made you think butter wouldn melt in her mouth. I din say what I was think. If I did I was sleep somewhere else for the night, no question about't.

"From now on," she says, "when you have an idea about my mother or these boys — or anything, Mister Felix, anything atall — I want you to come to me —*first.* Can you promise me that?"

Sure, sure. I nod ma head. Anything so she'll shut up and leamy alone and gimme some peace.

"Good!" she says, excited like before. "Then it's all settled! Puh-raise God!"

"Puh-raise God," I repeat-ed, think, Maybe that'll help, but I doan know. All this time, I ain't see no results yet.

"You sit there and enjoy your cigar, Mister Felix."

Oh, everything was hotsty-totsy then.

She was the craziest damn woman I ever met.

Tonight, when I come home from the shop, there was the ole lady set't the supper table. Din have much to say, but *smile,* plenty glad to see me, seemt to me.

Levi

Mizz Henrietta says I kin sing in the church choir, but I gotta practice, which is only natural, so we are on our way to church this evening.

Right nice out, sun down, cool, and not so many bugs as to bother a body.

Mizz Henrietta, she a happy soul. Got a little spring in her step.

But in the church at the choir practice, I see the strange way peoples is actin'. This one tells that one and that one tells the next one and on and on till the time comes Mizz Henrietta gets an earful same as the rest.

'Cept she don't pass it on. I am right beside her but she don't pass it on to me. She continues right on wid her singin'.

I kin see she is all red-eyed, and it ain't "Onward Christian Soldiers" that's done it. That one she likes right fine. Her singin' is off-key but she takes so much delight in that one that nobody says nothin' about it. They useta her voice, I reckon.

They laugh. Like most folk do wid Mizz Henrietta.

I thought we posta be singin'. But they's more whispers than they is singin', so this ain't hardly a good practice. I don't know what it is.

You gotta practice singin' if you wanna be good, if you got sumpn to work wid. That's what I do down in the holler. Cain't nobody hear me there.

Don't seem like singin's on anybody's mind tonight. Don't seem natural, whatever is in the air.

Seems like I am the last to be tole anything even though ole Hargrove says I am the first to know all.

But this time it ain't so. Hargrove got hisself in trouble, that much I kin make out. Bad enough he's on the white folks' team, they sayin'. But he done hit one of the white batters wid the ball.

Now we gotta have one in the choir, I hear them say plain enough.

Was me, they meant.

Mizz Henrietta, she stops in the middle of "Onward Christian Soldiers," slaps shut the songbook, and says, "Come, Levi, we must go home now," and picks up and leaves. Takes me by the hand. Don't bother to ixcuse herself. Don't talk to nobody on the way out. Ain't like her. Hargrove and me, we do that, we get a good talkin'-to.

I do like I'm tole. Leave the whispers behind.

I a black duck foll'ing its mama.

Choir practice is ovah for this evening.

Out on the dirt road Mizz Henrietta tells me, "Oh, that man. Men are just trouble. You are a boy still. But you too will change. I will never trust that race. Never have, never will."

She is tearful now. *Pulls* me to her. She a growed woman. Strong. I am jest a boy still.

"Walk in front," she says. "That way I can keep an eye on you." She lets go my hand and I do as I'm tole.

I cain't see how she's walkin' now, if she still has a spring in her step, but I don't dare turn around to look.

I think she is cryin' out loud.

Joe Blow

I ain't seen Old Man Peele's Buick out on the road or anywhere since a good two years before he died. When he took sick, the car went into the barn and stayed put. Peele didn't care about cars. Ran the hell out of that 'ere Ford when he was well. Both he and the Ford needed a rest, I reckon.

She was all shined up, the Buick. Looked like the first day she came from Flint. Run good too by the sound of her. Mizz Caledonia in the back seat with the daughter, that Henrietta. Nigger Lover behind the wheel. Was a sight you don't see every day.

Stopped the car on Main Street. Mizz Caledonia got out like she ain't seen a sick day in her life. Moved almost as good as Henrietta. Going to the beauty pollar.

The Eyetalian stayed with the car. Kept my eye on him. After a time, he got out of the car with a rag in his hand and stard to shine her up like she was hisn. Like you'd expect a nigger shoffer to do.

Maybe he's the Peele's nigger. Or shoffer. Or handyman. Nobody knows what-all he does out at the place.

Maybe that's why he's a nigger lover too, come to find out. He ain't no better than a damn nigger his own self. Like them two boys the Peeles got from the state. Them Peele women's the only legal slaveholders in this country in the Year of Our Lord nineteen hundred and thirty-five.

That was last Sattidy. This past week I made it my business to go out past the Peele place. I spied a coupley cars in the back, out by the barn. Reccanized Elwood Smitley's old Ford. Always th'owin' a rod, that car. Dewey Porter's Dodge he swears he'll go to his grave in. No sign of hide nor hair of *them*.

But the Eyetalian was out back in a work uniform, kind you see him wear at the packinghouse, hands and face all greazed up so's he looked like a monkey, head inside one motor, then t'other, 'cause he works on two cars at wunst.

(Some man. Don't do one car at a time. Does two at one time.)

This Sattidy, yesttidy, he was back in town. Just him this time, in that sporty little Dodge of hisn. Went to the barbershop. Will knows him. Will sees him a right smart. 'Cause when he ain't workin', the Eyetalian likes to get all slickered up. A ladies' man from what-all I hear. That foreign talk is what gets 'em, I reckon.

I was sittin', waitin' my turn behind Buck Langenfelder and Roger Humboldt. The two of them together can talk up a storm. While they're talkin', I'm watchin' Will. He has to use a lot of shampoo on that Eyetalian's hair, soaps it up real good, 'cause he's a greazy man. From the cars, I imagine, and the machines out at the packinghouse. Then he's got all that natural oil from his head like foreign people have. All that damn hair. If I's Will, I'd charge him extra to cut it.

Will and the Eyetalian strike up a conversation like they knowed one another all their lives. Will tells him he's seen the Peele place and the garden and this 'n' that and how he must have a green thumb. Like Old Man Peele when he was well and could do all that needed doin'.

"Can't you sit still?" Will asks him.

"Can't make no money that way," the Eyetalian says.

"I mean in the cheer," Will says. "You move around too much."

Will and the Eyetalian both find that funny.

The Eyetalian says he makes some money on the side fixin' cars. Car *re*pairs, he says. Says he fixed Old Man Peele's Buick to like she was new and the Ford's his next job.

"Wuddia do with all your money, Fee?" Will asks him. They on a first-name basis, them two. Not everybody comes in, is, with Will.

"Save it for a rainy day," the Eyetalian says. "Till some reech widow comes along to take care of me. You doan know any reech widows, do you, Will?"

"None come to mind," Will says, "but if I thinka one, I'll send her your way."

"By all means, be sure that you do."

"She ain't a widow," Will says, "but that Peele woman, Henrietta, she might help you out."

The Eyetalian smiles. "Who you kid, Will?"

Outa nowhere Buck Langenfelder pipes up. "Loves to sing, that woman. By God she does. You can hear outside the church sometimes. Big gal. Her voice carries."

That struck the Eyetalian funny, I don't know why.

"Damn shame she can't carry a tune," Roger Humboldt chimes in.

"Ain't that the God's truth," Buck says.

"Goin' to waste, that woman," Will says. "She might have some good years left in her, Fee. The bigger the gal, the better the lovin'. Has money to burn."

"But a tightwad, like her daddy," Buck lets everybody know.

The Eyetalian takes it all in. Looks like he's fallin' asleep in the cheer, but I seen that before. That's how he does.

Buck was never afraid to speak his mind for as long as I knowed him. Says to the Eyetalian, "You gotta grab it while you can. Strike while the iron is hot."

"Like to show her my hot arn," Roger says. "Wave it at her and let nature takes its course."

That gets a laugh out of Buck, so of course he has to say sumpn back. "Maybe if you was to get her after church, Mister. She's all het up after church."

"'Puh-raise God and bring me a man,'" Roger says.

That gets another laugh, but the Eyetalian don't even smile. Keeps his eyes shut. Acts like he don't hear. But he ain't missed a word.

Will's a-smilin', talks while he cuts. "She'd faint and when she came to she'd tell Fee here to pack his bags and git."

"Not if he was to kiss her down below," Roger says.

"Or put that big nose of hisn in it," Buck says. "That'd get her a-goin'."

That gets the biggest laugh yet, but the Eyetalian ain't even smilin', keeps his eyes closed. Smart man. The odds ain't in his favor.

Will don't want no trouble. Quick changes the suhject. "I think you fellers got it all wrong," he says. "That gal still has her cherry."

"That ain't so," Roger, Mister Know-All, says. "Your memory must be shot, Will. You mean to tell me you don't remember the actor fella she had out at the place awhile back?"

"I do," Will says real slow. "Now that you mention it, I do. There was even marriage talk, as I recall."

"Yeah, and I wonder who started that talk," Roger says, pleased to be right. "All that time out there, don't tell me he didn't get some."

"Free room and board is what he got," Will says. "*You* forget. The old lady was in the house. Still is for that matter."

"She was in a bad way even back then," Buck says. "She wouldna knowed what was what. Coulda been hanky-panky under her nose and she wouldna knowed."

Fellers talk. They didn't see what I saw last Sattidy.

"When the actor couldn't take it no more, he lit out," Will says. "Owed her plenty and broke her heart."

"Got another acting job," Buck says, "in another part of the country, is what I heard. Fella's gotta eat and I imagine he wore out his welcome out at the Peele place. Even actors gotta go where the work is, I reckon."

"Don't tell me he didn't get some," Roger says.

"If he did, he wouldna knowed what to do with it," Buck says. "Goddamn pansy actor, that's all he was."

"No matter, she's ripe," Will says. "Just hangin' from the vine. Waitin' for a young man like you, Fee."

"Not if you paid me," the Eyetalian says, his eyes wide open now like he just woke up and the idear never crosst his mind. "None of that stuff," he says. "Not me, Will. The other guy, maybe, but not me. I pay ma own way, come and go as I please."

"Just a joke, Fee."

I know Will: He don't think it's a joke. But he don't say no more, Will. Gets busy with his razor strop, fixin' to shave the Eyetalian. Will works for a livin', same as the rest of us Americans.

(I know too what Will thinks of men too lazy to shave theirselves.)

Me, I don't believe the Eyetalian for one minute. Bet he'd take that gal and all her and her family's got if she was to give him a tumble.

I know, I know. Just jokes amongst us fellers in the barbershop on a Sattidy afternoon. But many a true word said in a joke, many a true word.

Lulu

I give 'em all a good time, but Mitchell's got a smile there ain't no call for. He laughs, shuts his eyes. Man smiles with his eyes shut. Then it starts all over. Laughs again, eyes wide open.

"What's so funny?" Put my elbow in his side. "What's so funny, Mitchell? I don't hear Jack Benny."

"Can't a man laugh?" Then he laughs. A laugh like that, I don't trust.

"Time and a place for that," I told him. "What's it? Some more your schemes?"

"No schemes," he says, right pleased with himself. I hate a man that pleased with himself. But he pays. Knows which ones's got the jack too.

Usely.

That smile won't go away. I ain't no fool: I ain't gettin' any younger and I ain't gettin' any better.

I ain't ever seen Mitchell this happy before. Not where we are.

I said to him, "You ain't gonna tell me? Share your secret?"

He looks down to his bare chest. He's a skinny little man. His looks never got him nowheres.

"I told a certain party I wouldn't tell."

That's never stopped him before. "Everybody tells me," I said, "sooner or later."

He's got this big cockeyed grin. He likes it when we can do this. "I reckon that's so," he says, "and it ain't like there'd be any love lost between you and a certain party involved."

"Now I'm intrigued." Music to his ears.

He takes my hand away. No surprise there. I reckon he's only got so many in him.

"You want to hear my story or don't you?" he says.

"Sure, Mitchell," I said, "tell me your story."

He can't wait to tell it. He'd sooner that than anything. Like some women's husbands I get as trade.

"Baby Lawrence got herself in a family way."

So Junior was cut off. That's why he came to me.

"Already showin', that's why ain't nobody seen her," Mitchell says. Mister Know-All.

"You the papa," I said, "that how you know so much about it?"

That silly grin again. "Nope," he says, all happy at somebody 'sides his own self in the soup. Some folks are that way. "I ain't the papa," he says and I believe him.

I wisht I had or could do sumpn to make that silly grin go away. I wanted to crown him. "Then who's the papa if you ain't?" I said. "That Junior. Junior Somebody. He the one?"

Smiles back. "He is and he ain't."

Double talk. I told Mitchell: "Don't hold out on me."

"Name's Junior Williams. Buck Williams's son."

Means nothin' to me. "I don't know no Buck Williams."

"Nor will you ever make his acquaintance," Mitchell says. "Ain't like his son. Never paid for it in his life. Like Bart Lawrence, another party you ain't ever gonna meet."

The ways of the rich, I am thinkin'.

"So is he gonna marry that girl, that Baby Lawrence?"

"He's gonna do Bart Lawrence the favor," Mitchell says, "and marry his poor little knocked-up kid."

"He knocked her up, and he's gonna do Bart Lawrene a *favor?*"

"Bart Lawrence don't know that," Mitchell says. All smiles. "Man only knows what he's told. Junior knows damn well what would happen if the old man was ever to find out he's the daddy. Old Bart wouldn't give him the time of day before."

"And now?"

"And now he's in the family's bosom," Mitchell says. "But he'd be a dead man or as good as if word ever got out. Baby Lawrence knows that too and besides, a baby is the last thing that little gal wants. Ain't much more'n a baby her own self."

"So there ain't gonna be no baby?"

"There ain't gonna be no baby," Mitchell says. "It's all been arranged. I'm takin' Baby to New York to see a fella I know."

New York, I am thinkin', where she belongs. With the resta them heathens.

I admit I was curious. "So who's the old man think's the papa?"

Slaps his skinny thigh. He's about to bust. "This is where it gets good," he says. "You're gonna like this."

No I ain't Mitchell. I ain't gonna like it. I ain't liked anything so far, so why am I gonna like this?

"That nigger-lovin' wop is the papa and he don't even know it." Slaps his skinny thigh again. Giggles like a girl. There in my bed. "Don't even know Baby Lawrence."

"That's what you went and told Bart Lawrence?"

"Not me, Lulu. Why would that rich old gent ever listen to me unless it was to do a job he didn't want to do hisself? No, I didn't tell him. His darlin' daughter did."

"Baby Lawrence told the lie on the wop, to her daddy? She lied to her daddy and lied on the wop. What did she say?"

"Told her daddy the wop made her."

I came right out with it. "That's dirty. That's a damn dirty trick, Mitchell. On anybody, I don't care who."

Just *laughed*. Thought what he done was *hylarious*.

I asked him, "What's the old man gonna do?"

"He ain't a man to stand for it."

"You and Junior? Youse two made it up?"

"Mostly me," he says, prouda what he done. "But Junior hates niggers as much as me. Foreigners ain't far behind. Boy's no fool. He's set for life."

Shuts up, busy thinkin' how wonderful he is. Jiggers his leg, the one over the other, in the bed. Like a girl.

"That's his baby in her belly," I said. "You mean to tell me that don't make no diff'rence?"

"Don't make no diff'rence to Baby or to Junior," he says. "What's it to you, Lulu?"

Man don't forget a thing. I could shoot him right there in the bed. Do the world a favor. "They knew right where to come, didn't they?"

Says, "You oughta know, Lulu."

I oughta. I was in a family way when I met him. My own mother never spoke to me after that. My dear mother. Dead now too these many years.

Satisfied for now. Thinks he's put me in my place.

"You're just a jack-o'-all-trades, ain't you, Mitchell?"

"No call for you to get uppity, Lulu."

I let him talk. The son of a bitch can turn mean in a minute. Lucky for me, he wantsa talk.

"That ain't all," he says. "I ain't the only storyteller. Bart Lawrence'll have a pretty tale to tell anybody dumb enough to ask."

I don't give him time to play with it. "What might that be?"

"Right after I take Baby Lawrence to New York? She and Junior are gonna elope to Europe. Take a long boat ride. All on Daddy. Be away a couple months. At least a couple months. Come back mister-and-missus."

"Ain't life grand," I said. "What's gonna happen to that Felix?"

I see him once a week, sometimes more. Small town, you can't miss him. He's on the payment or else in that fancy car of hisn. Won't blow the horn, even if he's by himself. Oh, no, he's too polite, too much of a gen'leman for that. You can be right in front of him, and that man will not give you the time of day. I know there's ladies who like it thataway, but I ain't one of 'em. 'Sides, I wanna tell him about his draws and why I laughed. The sight of him can still make me laugh. But that stuck-up thing, he won't give me a tumble.

Mitchell takes his sweet time to answer.

"A man who forces his foul seed on the only daughter of Bart Lawrence?" Smiles that damn crooked smile. "I wouldn't want to be that wop for love nor money."

Shakes his head, laughs. His belly is like jelly.

After a while, he rolls over. Says, "Lulu," and I know what he wantsa do. Says, "Woman, you know you got a gray hair?"

But I don't take the bait. I won't give him the satisfaction. I won't give him an ixcuse to hit me tonight.

I hear his snores before I get up enough nerve to look over.

If I only had a gun.

Big Frankie

Looks down to me mean. Hands on my head.

Like he knows what I'm fixin' to say.

"I can't do it, Mitchell. What you want."

Looks mean to smile. Hands on my eahs. My hayer.

"Wuddia sayin', girlie?"

"Mister Felix. I can't make up no story."

Pulls on my hayer tighter. Pushes my head down.

"Did I say for you to stop?"

Nobody can see us. We're off to the side. In a hole. Mitchell knows places nobody else does.

"Do the belt."

I get it loose. He's a little man.

"You been a bad girl, ain't you?"

Why's he askin' me, I don't know.

"Wuddia reckon we're gonna haveta do about that?"

He's hurtin' my hayer.

"I can't do it. I can't. I'll make it up to you, Mitchell. Mitchell, d'you hear me?"

He don't hear me. Hands on my hayer. Tighter.

"Can't? Or don't want to? Which?"

"I ain't no liah. I can't lie, Mitchell. I can't. Please don't make me lie. I can't lie on that man."

"But you will," he says and pulls on my hayer. He pulls on my hayer like it's a chicken's neck.

"Gawhead girl," he says, "gawhead now. Don't be wastin' my time!"

He's screamin'. In a whisper. It's right loud where we are. In the hole.

I find it. He lets go my hayer then.

I hear somebody comin'. Singin'. Mister Felix.

"Hey there you, Meester Mitchell. I'm look for you. Come on, boy, get outa that hole. We got work to do. Now. Not next Christmas."

Mitchell pushes my head away *hard*. My hayer hurts the way he does it.

Zips his own self up. Pulls hisself outa the hole. Looks down, whispers, "Hear the rain, girlie?"

I hear the rain.

I feel my teeth.

I hate me too.

Felicissimo

Set in the car there. Pour down rain. Man, I mean buckets. Just bide ma time, wait for that girl, Francesa, I call her.

But she din act just right. Come out, stand there under the roof. She wouldn look to me.

So I knew some was up. Only stand to reason.

"Hey you Toots," I said to her, just for de'lment. "You walk home tonight and you gonna melt."

Lookt to me then. Smile. But she still wouldn come to me.

One woman there, Ginny or Jenny, I doan know which, she called to me:

"Hey, Fee-lix! Can't I go along for the ride?"

I din bother to answer. It ain't worth ma time.

Another woman there, Lena, she put in her two cents. Another one likes to talk. Between the two a-them, they doan miss much, I'll tellya right now.

"Yoo-hoo Fee-lix! Take me for a ride! Take me for a ride, Fee-lix. It's against the law to rob the cradle!" Another country heard from.

"I doan know whatchew talk," I said. Wouldn let on.

The other bigmouth, Ginny or Jenny, damn if I know her name, I doan care to know for that matter, she spoke up.

"Fee-lix, don't you know it's against the law to rob the cradle? Why don't you give us big girls a try? Don't us girls rate?"

Doan do no good to get mad 'cause those two, they'll keep it up. Once they think they got your goats up, they doan let go. Just the same, they are harmless, you midas well say. The two a-them struck me funny — this time.

"You're outa luck," I said. Play.

Come closer but was still under the roof. Both a-them was afraid to get wet.

"Whatsamatter, Fee-lix?" this Ginny says. "Can't you do three in one swat? I bet you can if you put your mind to it."

"He's gotta put more than his *mind* to it," Lena says.

Oh they thought that was funny. Laugh till they about bust their pissilstring. Almost fall down, laugh so hard. Both a-them. You'da thought Jack Benny tole a joke. I din see what was so funny.

I lookt to Francesa, that girl there. She wasn laugh. But she still wouldn look to me. If she din wanna ride all she hadda do was say so. I ain't hard to get along with. I was wait as courtesy more than anything else. That's all was. Was rain like hell.

"*Swat* ain't what *you* mean," Lena tells Ginny. She can barely spit't out, she's laugh so hard. Then the two a-them stard that cackle business. Cackle like hens.

I tole 'em, "Ma little car's too small for you two big girls." I hadda laugh maself. They ain't small by a long shot. But they din think that was funny.

"You mean we're too much woman for that little toy car," Ginny, she chimes in.

Was Lena's turn then. "Us girls," she says, "we like to play with *big* toys!" That stard them up again like nobody's business. Worse than before.

They was big girls all right. I guess they took't to heart what I mend as a joke. I din mean nothing by it, but they took't the wrong way. That's a woman for ya. They can deesh out all right but they can't take't.

Genly rule.

So I was set in the car there. Pour down rain. I toot ma horn to the girl there but she wouldn move. I said to her, "Hey you sis. Go, or stay?"

Lookt to me funny. Thought to maself, Suit yourself.

"Fee-lix." Was that Lena again. "I heard you was a man who gave growed women rides, not young girls!"

More a-that cackle business.

I din know what was wrong with that girl, Francesa. Finely she move-ed. Genly rule she's a pleasant somebody. Had women trouble, I guess. Damn if I know. I was just try to do somebody a favor. Din mean no more than that. Those two women there, Ginny and Lena, I know what they was think. But wasn so.

Francesa, she was move slow even in the pour down rain. Struck me funny. I never notice before but that kid din even have an umbrella. What was her mother think, send the girl to work like that? Rains once, twice a week. That toots there, she doan know no better. But her mother, *she* should have better sense. Doan have kids if that's the best you can do. That's how I feel about't.

Set in the car like somebody was hold a gun to her head.

I ask her, "What's wrong, sis? Doan feel good?"

"My teeth hurt," she says.

So that was the trouble. I knew was some.

"I'm sorry to hear," I said. "Whatchew take?"

"Nothin'."

"Uh-uh. That's no good. You should take some," I said. "Did you tell the nurse? She'll give you some."

"Nurse don't like me," she says.

"Who is she?" I said. "You go back in there and tell her you're sick. *Do like I tell you.* She'll give you some aspers. Aspers are good for headache, such as that."

"She said she'd report me if I give her trouble."

"This is sickness," I tole her. "You ain't cause trouble by be sick. Tell her you need some aspers. Wait here. I'll do for you, you want."

"No," she says, "they give me a bellyache."

I get some relief from, but not everbody is built like me. Everybody's machinery is diff'rent.

"I'll tellya what I'm gonna do," I said.

I took the pint I had in the glove compartment. Rye. Brand-new bottle. Broke the seal, unscrewed the cap, hand't to her.

"Doan swallow," I said, "'cause it'll make you sick sure enough. But swish around your mouth real good. Wherever your teeth hurts. For a minutes or two. Then spit it out. Do it again when you go home. Just doan swallow."

She took't. "At home," she says, "they'll think I'm drunk."

"No they woont," I said, "not if you do like I'm tellin' you. Mi' smell like. But you ain't if you doan swallow."

She did like I tole her, open the door to spit, and I forgot all about those two damn bitches there doan miss a thing. They raised so much hell you was think the world was come to an end.

"So that's how you do it, Fee-lix. Now we know. You get 'em drunk first."

"Shame on you, Fee-lix. Rob the cradle's one thing. But this kid's under sixiteen! Damn you."

"Damn you is right. We thought you was better. But you're just like the rest around here."

The idea! It never crosst ma mind, what they was think. I swear it din.

"Oh, you doan know whatchew talk," I said. I was mad. "Go to the devil! Both a-you."

I lookt to Francesca. She was look better already.

"Toots," I said, "you heard them women. About ready to eat me alive. I take you home I'll never hear the end of it. I can't take you home today. But that'll help you some, I bleeve."

Back seat I had ma umbrella. She took ma umbrella, ma pint; got out the car and starda walk. Was still pour down rain.

I put ma car in *re*verse, to where those two women was stand. Rolled down the window. Wanda make sure they heard me.

"Youse two," I tole 'em, "are the dirtiest damn women as I ever met."

They din say a word that time.

Then I put ma car in gear and I went right straight home.

I had enough damn foolishness for one day.

Daggett

He's got his backside in a cheer in my office.

"So much for your plan," I says.

"Shit," he says. "Bitched by women again." Because it's never his fault when the bottom falls out. A lying, scheming son of a bitch.

Family, I have to remind myself ever so often.

"Bad luck," I tell him. "All you Mitchells got it."

"Don't I know it," he says. "Them bitches. I got Mother Nature on my side. I got the two biggest busybodies knowed to man. I got the wop with the gal in the car and givin' her a bottle to boot."

"You forget," I says, trying to keep a straight face, "the healing power of hooch."

"Wop's one lucky bastard," he says.

"No, he ain't," I says. "He's about as unlucky as poor Cousin Pooch. Off the job six months now."

Laughs. "You been keeping track?"

"My old woman's been keeping track."

"I can't tell you how much he's missed at work," he says.

"Don't even try," I says. "Tell my old woman about your plan. She was all set to miss his dog's face at the supper table five-six times a week."

"Now C.C.," he says, "I didn't go and put *all* my eggs in one basket. You take your chances with a simp. No, I got another plan to get Pooch back on his feet."

I knew the plan. Ain't just women can't keep a secret. I let him tell it anyways. Knew it all except when.

"Tonight," he says, "after supper."

"You know, Billy," I says, "you have what they call a sixth sense about folks."

"You think so, C.C.?"

"Know it for a fact," I says. Waiting for him to catch up with it. "I got a visitor today. Hadda go to Oakland to pick him up off the train."

He's right innarrested now. "Must be a pretty important fella for you to leave town," he says.

"He is, all right," I says, watching him get curiouser and curiouser, a sight to see.

"Ain't you gonna tell me who?"

"Federal marshal," I tell him.

"What brings him here?"

"Hot on the trail of some murder suspect. Italian man. Think he killed another man in his apartment, fight over some woman, and then ran out. In Cincinnati. Last winter."

His face is all changed. Got his feet down off my desk. "You stall him," he says, his mind working as fast as it can, "stall him till morning. I'll get the job done right this time."

"That don't make sense." I tell him. Like I'm talking to a sane man. His side of the family, they're all the same. Got what folks around here call a crazy streak. "Why not let the federal fella take him away? Leave him the dirty work?"

"You don't understand, C.C. It ain't just about what he done to Pooch and tryin' to do to me and what Bart Lawrence thinks he done to his Baby. We don't want folks to forget what happens, they get idears like hisn. What he started, it's bigger'n one man. We got to kill off the idears too."

I can see it's no use. "Till morning," I says, "but then it's my turn."

Charles

After supper, we was only too glad to stand up and walk. Headed out towards the barn. Fee gimme a cigar. We're both smokin'. Fee makin' fun.

"Praise the Lord," he was sayin', "and send me a man."

"Mizz Henrietta's the least of your worries," I said. "For a quiet fella, Fee, you sure know how to stir the pot."

"Oh how you talk," he says. "What did I do?"

"What *ain't* you done?" I said.

Shrugs. "That boy Levi, he's a singer. That boy Hargrove, he's a ballplayer. I made a suhgestion and now I got a black mark against me. That's too damn bad."

"You left out Baby Lawrence," I said.

"I doan know whatchew talk," he says. Serious.

"You mean to tell me you don't know Baby Lawrence?"

Shakes his head. "No-I-do-not. Should I know her?"

"She says you do. Says you did her."

"*I* did her?"

"That's what she says. Says you forced yourself on her. That's big trouble, Fee, if it's true."

"That's her story. I doan know nobody by that name."

"She ain't been seen lately," I said. "Some folks think she's jammed."

"Maybe so, but not by me, she ain't. What the hell kinda name is that for a woman anyhow?"

"Around here," I said, "her daddy's name is the one folks remember. Bart Lawrence."

"Never met him," he says. "What's his line?"

"You name it," I said. "If there's a nickel to be made, he's Johnny on the spot."

"Hoo-ray for him," he says. "But I doan know him or his baby daughter, and anybody says some else is a damn liar. That's all there is to it. I swear, some people. *Hello, you Queenie. Hello, you Tess.*"

The two dogs run up. Licked his face, licked his hands.

"You let Mizz Henrietta's dogs go free?" I said.

"Oh no," he says, "they get out on they own. Some way, I ain't feegured out how. Two pretty smart girls. You should see Cholly, when I come home from the job? There they are, wait for me, best pals, shake-a-tail, shake-a-tail. Carry on, make you think they're liable to eat you up. But they woont."

"They sure know you," I said.

"They ma shadow," he says and pulls two chicken bones from his shirt pocket and gives each bitch one. "Gotta look out for ma friends, y'know."

"You sure do know how to stir the pot," I said.

"Who, me?" he says. "Uh-uh. No sir, not me."

It was the dogs saw 'em first. Didn't stop to consider the odds, I reckon. Just let out a ferocious yelp, left their bones and rushed 'em. Fee was right: They sure made like they could eat you up. Fee stood up then, and he saw it about the same time I did: first the sheets, then the flames, a red sky. He had no more turned around when the dogs went down: fast. The first one kicked, then shot; the other'n shot on the run. When they went down we made a run for Fee's Dodge.

"Let me drive," I said.

"Why you?" he says.

"'Cause that's my line," I said.

He th'owed me his keys and we drove with out heads down, zig-zagged all over the field, I don't know why they didn't hit the tars or shoot us dead. Pure luck, I thought till we was out on the hard road and looked back and saw how busy they was with their flames. You couldn't see the grape arbor or the rosebushes or the vegetable patch for the flames.

We went a ways, two miles, maybe three, and there was s'more of 'em. Dozens of 'em. In sheets, with torches, flames everywhere.

And behind me, his breath on my neck, that boy Levi.

Felicissimo

We din have no time or else sure enough we was take that boy home and let Miss Prucey there warm his backside. Those fellas, all dress up, think they own the country, was right behind.

Big shots. Thought they was anyhow.

I gave Cholly the signal, and justthatquick he made a turn, and *down* we went or else they was keel us and and that boy too. No question about't.

Ma good friend Mitchell, I thought to maself.

Cholly that rascal he drove ma car on the road, off the road till the axle she went bye-bye. When we couldn go no fuhther I tole Cholly, that boy, both: "Do what I tell you now: I wange you stay put. This ma trouble, not yours. I doan wange you get mix up. Savvy?"

I slam-banged the door and off I went. I went a little way and damn if I din hear some behind me. I quick took a look and just as I thought. Was that damn boy. Levi. Those boys neither one liss worth a damn when you say some. In one ear and out the other.

"Whattadahell," I said. Stop. "Din I tell you to stay in the car? You'll be safe if you stay with that white man. *Now go on git before I lose ma temper.*"

I ran like hell 'cause I was lose time talk. But damn it to hell, when I lookt outa the cawner of ma eye, I saw sure enough he was run behind me again. I din have no time to stop and talk or else I would.

I was down by the river on the sand there when I heard the shots and felt the one. What happ after that, I couldn tell you.

I woke up on the other side of the river. Sun shine so bright off the sand was hurt your eyes. Ma clothes was dry. I was feel pretty damn good. Starda walk up the heel to the road.

Halfway up I heard a car come along. So I got behind a tree. Whoever was saw me. Stopped the car.

Who was but Red. All dress up in her Sunday clothes. In ma car from home. All fix up, shine so pretty.

She called to me: "You're just the man I'm looking for."

"Hey you Redhead," I said, "what's the idea?"

"Wanna ride in my new car?" she said, smile so wide.

"Look mighty fameelyer," I said. "Where's Roberto?"

"Went home," she said. I din know what she mend by that. Din ask. "I went to Baltimore," she said.

"Baltimore do you some good?" I ask her.

"Too far gone," she said. "So here I am."

"Where are we, Red?" 'Cause I din know.

Lookt to me, laugh. "Don't you know, Fee?"

"If I knew," I said, "I wouldn ask."

"Bull's eye," I heard somebody say. "Good work," some damn fool said. Another big shot spoke up. "Leave him for the buzzards." Then that boy Levi was talk.

"Git home," I said, "before I fan your backside."

He din move. Said some I couldn quite make out. Was cry.

"Stop that foolishness," I said. "You can visit, but I ain't gonna talk to you."

Spoke pretty plain then: "I'll put you in the river."

I din say no more. What was the use to argue? Red was wait. Blow the horn. One time, two times.

"Doan rush me," I said, "I'ma come."

"So's Christmas," she said.

Oh, she gave me a big hug. Smell so good, I swear I never smell anything better.

"See here, young lady," I said, "you got me outa bed before breakfast this morning."

She was *laugh.* "I brought lunch," she said. Had a picnic basket beside her.

So off we went. Ma chariot never ran so smooth, never sound so sweet. If you din know better you was swear it had wings.

Hargrove

Good thing they left the barn out here or else I wouldn't have no place to pitch my games. Yeah, they left this barn and all that Mizz Henrietta's daddy owned; burnt up all that was the new man. Did the job right, some folk say.

I know you cain't hardly tell he was here, the way things looks now.

You don't see much of Mizz Caledonia. She back upstairs. I see her lookin' out the winda from time to time. Act like she don't see me. Mister Charles gone too. He got a stern warnin' from the town folk. Since then he ain't been back. Cain't nobody blame him.

Levi, he sticks close by when he ain't downta river. Had a doctah lookidum. 'Cause they think he hit his head on sumpn 'cause he talks more crazy than befo'.

I tole 'em he was always that way. Evah since I been knowin' him.

If I was to say what I think, there ain't no tellin' what they mighta done wid him. That nigger's lucky he wudn't shot dead.

Course he ain't in the church no mo'. For a long time he wouldn't even sing. Then one day he was out here wid me and it come back to him.

Here's how crazy he is:

He tells me the Eyetalian man's in the river. Says he put him there.

"Well, he's a goner then," I says. "'Cause the man, he cain't swim."

"How do you know so much?" Levi says.

That Dumbhead. "'Cause he tole me so, that's how."

Most folks, they say the buzzards got him. But ain't nobody found a body chet. Even confounded the federal fella. Had some men swim the river. All they got was wet.

My guess is he's way down yonder. Feesh dinner.

"If you kin keep a secret," I says, "I'll tell you who he was."

So Levi, he took a solemn swear and I tole him.

Well, that boy laughed and laughed and laughed like it was me who was crazy. I ain't said a word to nobody. 'Specially now, the way he is. Boy smiles allatime. Sings like befo'. Hear him?

"Fiammifero, fiammifero ..."

That's sumpn to do wid a match, a spark, a flame. Leastways that's what Mister Groucho Marx tole us, if you kin believe anything that man said.

Strike three! Game over. Our side wins.

The End

Printed in the United States
By Bookmasters